A Thousand Years

By Julie Shurley

A Thousand Years

© Copyright 2025 by Julie A. Shurley
julieshurley1@gmail.com

All rights reserved.
No portion of this book may be reproduced in any form, except for brief quotations in reviews, without the written permission of the publisher.

Scripture quotations are from the New King James Version (NKJV).

Cover design: Julie Shurley
Cover art: Kevin Carden
Illustrated by Neena Sansonetti

Printed in the United States of America

Dedication

Many thanks to my students, many of whom inspired me to write this story, and many more who heard me read it for the first time and encouraged me to publish this book. I thank my family for their help and support; for listening, critiquing and providing editing suggestions. Thanks to the many friends who helped edit the manuscript. Thanks to my son Cameron who wrote the last chapter of this book addressing the misunderstanding of God's character that a mistaken view of hell fire brings. Most of all, I thank my loving Creator and Friend, Jesus, for giving me His Spirit to guide in the writing of this, His story.

Table of Contents

Forward   5
Preface   8

I.	The Blessed Hope Realized	12
II.	The Sea of Glass	21
III.	What Might Have Been	28
IV.	Who is Your God?	36
V.	Tears in Heaven	44
VI.	Joy in Heaven	51
VII.	Ransomed	57
VIII.	Healing Our Brokenness	65
IX.	Before the Throne	75
X.	The Court of the Universe	82
XI.	The End of a Thousand Years	88

The Controversy Ended   99
God Unframed   108
The Millennium:
    What Does the Bible Say?   119

Forward

Sitting in my chair at morning worship my thoughts wallowed in deep discouragement. Failure again. Disappointment - again. The old sins, new sins, and apparently-not-overcome sins surfaced again. From utter despair and shame, I prayed a simple plea with the last bit of faith I could muster, "God, if You believe in me and want me to change, show me something of Your power and give me something to believe in."

With doubt and undefined hopelessness I began one of the most amazing journeys I have ever experienced - Jesus! As that dark week in my freshman year unfolded, the pages of a life changing book opened. From its pages the author, doubling as my speech teacher, brought to life an unmatched panorama of the completion of the Great Controversy - The millennium: The thousand years in heaven. Spanning from the catastrophic completion of Earth's sinful history to the recreation of a perfect world void of any trace of sin, the theme of Jesus' love rings over all tears, confusion, and the sins recorded in the book.

As it traces you as the main character, you find yourself engrossed in something only your mind can imagine and experience: a relationship with Christ. Moving through those 1,000 years with Christ face-to-face, you experience Him on a completely new level, the level of physical closeness and real visible interaction.

From the pages of this blessed book, I experienced a new joy and previously unattainable excitement: Heaven. From it's excellent authorship the experiences of the human race collide with the divine in an epic and yet graceful anticipated retelling of your own experience.

If you truly want to break the chains of this world, experience Jesus and have Him change your life, this book gives you a glimpse of what heaven may be like. I can't wait to be there. I want to see you there too. Let this book change your life like it did my own!

~Caleb Brooks - Class of '25

A Thousand Years is a gripping portrayal of what God's redeemed may experience in that long-awaited Millenium after Jesus returns and takes His children home. The depiction of Heaven in all its glory and splendor will exhilarate you as you read of what it may be like to be in the very presence of God Himself, converse with Jesus, meet your Guardian Angel and others you have read about in the Bible, and to be reunited with friends and family.

Similarly, the poignant and likely stories of lost loved ones will tug at your heartstrings. Our decisions today have eternal consequences.

This book can recalibrate and refocus your heart and mind on the eternal things that matter if you prayerfully ask God to help you do that. No doubt, you will want to share this book with others. Bravo, Julie! Thank you for allowing God to use you to evoke in us an imperative reality check before it is too late by the application of the truths God has so graciously given us.

~Anna Chiarenza

Preface

Heaven has long been a favorite study of mine. I love to read the descriptions in the Bible and the writings of Ellen White and contemplate what it must be like to be there. Jesus promised us:

"In my Father's house are many mansions. I go to prepare a place for you, and if I go and prepare a place for you, I will come again and receive you to myself, that where I am, there ye may be also."
John 14:3

We are told that we should let the imagination dwell upon heavenly realities. This exercise will keep the invisible, eternal things before us so that the visible, temporal things of this world around us will not seem so enduring; so important.

"Jesus has brought heaven to view, and presents its glory to our eyes in order that eternity may not be dropped out of our reckoning. With eternal realities in view we will habitually cultivate thoughts of the presence of God. This will be a shield against the incoming of the enemy; it will give strength and assurance, and lift the soul above fear."

"If He can fasten the mind upon the future life and its blessedness, in comparison with the temporal concerns of this world, the striking contrast is deeply impressed upon the mind, absorbing the heart and soul and the whole being.

"Jesus comes to present the advantages and beautiful imagery of the heavenly, that the attractions of heaven shall become familiar to the thoughts, and memory's hall be hung with pictures of celestial and eternal loveliness..." *Last Day Events* by Ellen White p 284

After attempting to relate a vision of heaven, Ellen White found herself at a loss to put into words the wonders she had seen and exclaimed:

"The wonderful things I there saw I cannot describe. Oh, that I could talk in the language of Canaan, then could I tell a little of the glory of the better world.

"Language is altogether too feeble to attempt a description of heaven. As the scene rises before me, I am lost in amazement. Carried away with the surpassing splendor and excellent glory, I lay down the pen and exclaim, 'Oh, what love! What wondrous love!' The most exalted language fails to describe the glory of heaven or the matchless depths of a Saviour's love.

"If we could have but one view of the celestial city, we would never wish to dwell on earth again." Ibid p 287

The story you are about to read sprang from my burning desire to see those I have labored with and prayed for, saved in heaven. My thoughts encompassed the unbearable possibility that some dear ones may not be there. Realizing this, it occurred to me that this time we call the millennium is a bit different than the rest of eternity. During this thousand years, we will have the opportunity to ask all of those uncomfortable questions; time to dispel possible mis-conceptions of God's character; time to heal from the wounds our spirits have suffered from the trauma of earthly life.

I have several goals in writing this story:
1. To stay as true to inspiration and life experiences as possible
2. To bring to view a vivid picture of the eternal world
3. To examine the purpose of the millennium
4. To reveal the beauty of God's character, and
5. To impress the reader of the infinite grace of Christ and the serious consequences of rejecting His mercy.

In order to do this, I have drawn upon my experiences with many of the people I have known and worked with. I have spent many years teaching and mentoring young people. Over the years I have "adopted" many kids who still call me "mom" and I pray for these precious young people every day. The characters in this story are based upon real people or a combination of real people in order to make the story true to life. In doing so, I do not want to give the impression that I am telling the stories of these people through the characters in this story. If you recognize yourself, or someone you know in a character, just remember that many people have similar struggles and similar choices to make. I have also chosen to include you, as the reader, in my story. This is only for the purpose of drawing you into the solemn contemplation of the eternal consequences of your decisions. It is not intended to predict your destiny.

As you read, please engage your imagination. Close your eyes if you need to, and allow the words you read to paint vivid pictures in your mind. I want you to feel as though you are experiencing the things you are reading. May the Spirit of God fill your mind and heart, is my prayer.

~Julie Shurley

I.
The Blessed Hope Realized

*For the Lord Himself will descend from heaven with a shout,
with the voice of an archangel, and with the trumpet of God.
And the dead in Christ will rise first.
Then we who are alive and remain
shall be caught up together with them in the clouds
to meet the Lord in the air.
And thus we shall always be with the Lord.
1 Thessalonians 4:16-17*

Everything had been dark and filled with chaos. The final death throes of the earth had been violent and terrifying, but now, NOW everything was LIGHT! I had to pinch myself to believe this was real. But there could be no doubt. I was bathed in brilliant white light and beside me was a beautiful, kind being who I instinctively realized was my guardian angel. As I looked around, I could see many of my dear friends, some I hadn't seen in a long time. We caught each other's gazes and they too bore expressions of wonder and joy.

"Mama!" As I turned to see who called, I was suddenly enveloped in a bear hug and lifted off my feet. It was Ari, his face aglow with joy. I was so glad to see him! Many and earnest had been my prayers on his behalf. "My dear son!" I was too overcome to say more.

"You never stopped praying for me, did you, Mom? I know that's why I'm here - because of your prayers and God's mercy!"

"Ari, I want to hear everything that happened after we lost contact." I wanted to talk right then, but there wasn't time. There were so many dear ones to greet! But, we would have eternity to catch up! There would be time.

Several more of my children - by birth and "adoption" - came running to me and we embraced in relief and overwhelming joy to be together. I looked up to see Andrew, a brilliant smile shining from his ebony face. What a precious young man. I was delighted, but not surprised to see him here. Tony and Scott edged their way through the press to join us, and over on the far side of the cloud I could see my father caught in a tangle of happy friends.

I gave my mother's hand a squeeze as she stood beside me, and my husband drew me close, his arm about my waist. I looked into their faces. Gone were the lines of suffering and distress that had so recently etched their countenances. The last several months had been marked by sleepless nights, agonizing prayers, soul searching, and emotional trauma for each of us. What an incredible relief it was to now realize our "blessed hope" for which we had waited with such enduring expectation!

It was quite a while before I began to look around a bit more in this company of bright, happy travelers. We were almost to the pearly gates of the heavenly city and I had enjoyed many hours conversing with my angel, my family, and friends, both old and new. But a sudden twinge of apprehension played at the corners of my mind as I wandered through the milling cloud of happy people. I had not caught sight of you. Come to think of it, there were several people I hadn't seen yet. "Well, there were untold thousands here," I assured myself. Surely I would see you once we were standing on the sea of glass.

I could not stop gazing in wonder at the throne in the center of the cloud. Jesus, my precious, awesome Redeemer and King was right there! Now and then, I caught His eye, and my heart felt like it would burst, or melt. The singular love I felt from His gaze was something I cannot even describe with words. I thought I could just BE in His presence for all eternity and never feel the need for anything else.

We had been traveling through space for several days, and now we drew near the Orion Nebula. Expansive, glowing clouds encircled us, funneling us toward an exceedingly bright opening ahead.

We were entering Orion's portals, more enormous and grand than I could have ever imagined! I could see nothing distinct in the brilliant light for some time, but as we drew nearer, I began to make out a majestic gateway with two leaves of iridescent pearl. High golden walls extended in either direction and atop these walls were sentinel angels.

As we drew near to the city of God, the challenge was given by our escorting angels, "Lift up your heads, O ye gates, and be lifted up, you everlasting doors, that the King of Glory may come in!" Joyfully the waiting sentinels responded, "Who is this King of Glory?" Of course, they already knew, but they wanted to hear the answer of exalted praise for their King. "The Lord, strong and mighty! The Lord, mighty in battle! Lift up your heads, O ye gates; Even lift them up, ye everlasting doors; and the King of Glory shall come in!"

Again I heard the challenge, "Who is this King of glory?" The angels never tire of hearing His name exalted. Once again, the escorting angels replied, "The Lord of hosts, He is the King of glory." Psalm 24:7-10. {Adapted from White, *The Desire of Ages* p 833}

Then the gates swung back and I watched as this vast throng of happy people filed in through those magnificent pearly gates. Songs of triumph mingled with the music from angel harps till heaven seemed to overflow with joy and praise. Love has conquered. God's children have been ransomed from the land of the enemy. Heaven rang with a magnificent anthem of praise. "Blessing, and honor, and glory, and power, be unto Him that sits on the throne, and to the Lamb forever and ever." Revelation 5:13. {Adapted from White, *The Desire of Ages* p 835}

My Missing Children

I was enraptured. But I watched carefully to see you somewhere. My guardian angel was looking at me, following my intent gaze. Knowing me all too well, he read the question in my eyes before I could bring myself to ask it. Finally, my eyes met his, and with a sickening feeling, I knew the answer by the look in his eyes. "Not here?" I whispered. He sadly shook his head. "What about Kelly, I haven't seen her either, or Rachel... Gabe? Mark?" Each question received the same answer.

I began to cry as my angel gently put his arm around me. There were people here who I would never have imagined would be ... why not these precious young people I had worked with, taught in class, had in my home? With some, I had spent hours in heart-felt conversations about life, God, commitment... their struggles to overcome sin, addictions, the attractions of the world. I had spent many early mornings and sometimes sleepless hours of the night in earnest, agonizing prayer for their salvation. I had trusted, hoped, clung to God's promises that He would finish the work He had begun in their hearts.

Promises like Philippians 1:6 - "being confident of this very thing, that He who has begun a good work in you will complete it until the day of Jesus Christ;" And Isaiah 49:25 - "But thus says the Lord: 'Even the captives of the mighty shall be taken away, And the prey of the terrible be delivered; For I will contend with him who contends with you, And I will save your children.'"

Lost in my thoughts I became unaware of the joyful scene before me. I vividly recalled a conversation I had with Mark. He was such a fun-loving kid, and yet, he had a very serious, earnest side. It was at the end of class; I could tell something was bothering him and I asked him what was going on. Things were not going well, he confessed. Sensing something deeper than the struggles with school and friends that he described, I asked him how his spiritual walk was going.

"Not good" He let out a long sigh as he examined his shoestrings. I waited for him to continue.

"I know what's right...and I know if I want to follow God there are things in my life I need to give up, but I don't want to."

"Mark," I asked, "what are these things you are holding onto that are more important to you than Jesus?"

"Oh, things like music, movies, video games... and other things... and really, I'm scared of what I might do if I don't surrender these things to Jesus, but I just don't want to let go of them."

"But ... why?"

"I like them too much. My music, the videos I like, they make me feel something. Spiritual things just don't hold that kind of attraction for me. They're dull - they don't speak to me."

"Mark, it's these very things that are destroying your interest in spiritual things. You are being held in bondage!"

"I know… I'm in bondage by my own choice, I guess." He concluded with a joyless chuckle.

I pleaded with him to surrender those cheap pleasures, so destructive to his life and happiness, and give himself wholly to God. I assured him the reward was well worth the sacrifice. He looked at me with tear-brimmed eyes. He seemed so totally miserable, and yet, he could not, would not surrender. I prayed with him and told him I would keep praying.

He had seemed better after that. He gave beautiful talks in church, taught Bible School class… Eventually he moved on and it seemed he was doing well. Last I knew he was working with a ministry. I thought surely he had made things right with God.

And then there was Gabe, dear Gabe. He had stayed in our home for a while. We all loved him. We were privileged to see him make his commitment to God public by baptism. He certainly had his struggles with temptation. He fought hard battles against self. When he sang in the church choir, I could imagine his rich bass joining with the angel choir … someday. After he moved out, we were so proud of him for his determination to follow God's call on his life. He was always in my prayers. Slowly over time, we lost contact. But I never doubted that God would use him mightily.

II.
The Sea of Glass

And I saw something like a sea of glass mingled with fire, and those who have the victory over the beast, over his image and over his mark and over the number of his name, standing on the sea of glass, having harps of God.
Revelation 15:2

My thoughts suddenly came back to the present as I was swept on by the throng entering the gates. Jesus was at the head of the procession. He led the way to a shimmering plain that resembled ice, yet beneath it, or reflected from it (I could not tell which) were flames of fire dancing and flickering in all the colors of the rainbow. This area was vast, but I could clearly see every person as we made a hollow square around its perimeter. A look overhead took my breath away. There were high arches that looked as though they were made of transparent metal. The arches were higher than the glassy area was across. Dazzling light shone through and flooded the glassy sea with intense brilliance. Angels flew gracefully around, guiding heaven's new family members to their places in the vast square. My family members stood on each side of me, their faces beaming.

I watched as angels flew from the far side of the sea of glass carrying glittering crowns. How beautiful, I thought. She would have looked beautiful with one of those crowns on her head...

My mind drifted to Kelly, beautiful Kelly. I'm a mother of boys. But Kelly was the first girl that ever stole my heart. She was like a lost child. Insecure, frightened, stubborn - my, was she stubborn. I spent so many hours with her, reassuring, correcting, encouraging her to move forward. I prayed with her regularly and studied the Bible with her. Slowly she began to do life on her own. She needed less of my time and attention. I suppose that's as it should have been. But I never stopped praying for her. Not here? I squeezed my eyes shut, willing the realization to be disproved. Hoping that this scene might be only a dream... maybe there was really more time and things could be different. How could there be such joy and happiness and at the same time such heartbreaking disappointment? I just could not cope with this huge emotional dichotomy; I felt I was going to faint.

My angel was again beside me. He gently brushed away a stray tear. His gentle voice soothed my conflicted feelings as he said, "Remember, He is your exceeding great reward." He pointed to Jesus standing in the middle of the sea of glass. He was glorious to behold, dressed in royal robes shimmering in the brilliant light. He was tall! Much taller than 21st century people. But as I watched, a being emerged from the crowd and as he walked toward the Savior, I could see he was nearly as tall himself! There was an audible gasp of wonder and anticipation from the thousands of the redeemed around the perimeter.

Adam

This was Adam! The Son of God walked toward him with outstretched arms to receive the father of our race—the being whom He created, who sinned against his Maker, and for whose sin the marks of the crucifixion are borne upon the Savior's form. As Adam recognized the prints of the cruel nails, he could not bring himself to embrace his Lord, but in humiliation he cast himself at His feet, crying, "Worthy, worthy is the Lamb that was slain!" Tenderly the Savior lifted him to his feet and directed him to look over the Eden home from which he had so long been exiled.

I watched the expression of transported joy as he looked at the trees that were once his delight,—the very trees whose fruit he himself had gathered in the days of his innocence and joy. He recognized the vines that his own hands had trained, the very flowers that he once loved to care for. He looked as if in a dream, unable to grasp the reality of the scene; but then the comprehension dawned upon him that this was indeed Eden restored, more lovely now than when he was banished from it. The Savior led him by the hand to the tree of life and picking some of

23

the glorious fruit, gave it to him to eat. Adam looked around him, taking in the multitude of his family redeemed, standing in the Paradise of God. Then he cast his glittering crown at the feet of Jesus and fell into his Redeemer's embrace. (Adapted from White, *The Great Controversy* p 647-648)

Receiving a Crown of Life

Now Jesus moved down the line of saints. On each head, He was placing a crown with His own hands. I watched Him move from one to the next, trembling with anticipation as He drew ever nearer to where I stood. As I saw Him placing crowns, heavy with stars, upon my sons' noble heads, I could hardly see a thing for the tears of joy that streamed down my face. How utterly grateful I was! What a rich reward to be able, by God's grace, to see my children receiving a crown of life!

And then ... My Savior stood before me. Time stood still. I looked into His eyes - my breath left me. An immense wave of unfathomable love washed over me - no, through me. I was enveloped in love itself. I can't even explain it. Nothing like the cheap feelings we called love on earth. Even parental love, or the committed love between husband and wife pale in comparison to what I felt in that moment. He spoke, and His voice was a rich deep velvet. Its resonance warmed my whole being. He spoke my name, but it was not the same name I was known by on earth. When He spoke it, the sound was very familiar to my ears and very personal.

"I'm so glad you are here," He said, "I have waited with longing expectation for this day when I could see you face to face. Welcome home!" I just smiled, speechless. I saw Him take a crown from an angel's hands and, as He reached out to place it upon my head, I could see the scars - the nail prints in his hands. Tears sprang to my eyes again. I had caused those. My sins had wounded Him, and yet He loved me and welcomed me to His home forever.

Before I knew it, He had moved on. We each received a palm branch, a gem stone with our new name engraved on it, and a harp. We were escorted into a magnificent dining hall and seated around a gorgeously laid table. Jesus served us each Himself and we all drank the new wine together - the first time in over two thousand years for Jesus. He explained that He had been waiting to drink it with us since the supper before His death when He drank the cup with His disciples.

As the meal ended, we joined the angels in a very special hour of worship in the presence of God the Father, the Son, and the Spirit. We all played our harps in perfect harmony and sang this new song as though from memory!

Our Heavenly Home

I cannot describe all the things we did and enjoyed together over the next few days. We drank from the river of life that flowed forth from the eternal throne. We walked beside the river flowing through a grassy meadow full of flowers. This was Eden, Adam and Eve's first home, preserved from the earth before it was destroyed by the flood. In the midst of it grew the magnificent tree of life, its mighty trunk rooted to each bank of the river and uniting into one as it towered hundreds of feet into the air. We picked its beautiful fruit and marveled at its delicious flavor. We were amazed time after time by the sights and sounds as we toured this heavenly place.

New insights and understanding of things long obscured to my feeble brain literally blew my mind! I had a long conversation with my guardian angel and many things that had troubled me in my experiences came into focus as he explained the activities behind the scenes. It all made sense now. Except ....

"All that has perplexed us in the providences of God will in the world to come be made plain. The things hard to be understood will then find explanation. The mysteries of grace will unfold before us. Where our finite minds discovered only confusion and broken promises, we shall see the most perfect and beautiful harmony. We shall know that infinite love ordered the experiences that seemed most trying. As we realize the tender care of Him who makes all things work together for our good, we shall rejoice with joy unspeakable and full of glory." White, *Testimonies to the Church* vol. 9 p 286 par. 2

III.
What Might Have Been

The heart is deceitful above all things,
And desperately wicked; Who can know it?
I, the Lord, search the heart, I test the mind,
Even to give every man according to his ways,
According to the fruit of his doings.
Jeremiah 17:9-10

As the days passed, I began to ponder more and more the sad reality that so many people I had hoped would be here were not. Rachel, for instance. She had spent a lot of time in our home. Rachel was the kind of person that spoke her mind and asked deep questions. She wasn't shallow like so many girls her age. She held opinions that perhaps were not always in line with the expected norms in a conservative Christian community, but she was nonetheless, very sincere in her search for truth. We had a lot of conversations about life, Christianity, the role of women in the church, politics. It was always very mentally stimulating to talk with her. Her sincerity and love for the Lord were very evident, I thought. She went on to attend Bible college, took an education major, and after graduating, she took a call to teach in one of our mission schools. What could have happened? I was sure of her commitment to Christ!

The more I pondered, the more troubled I became, and finally, I spoke with my angel again. I did not want to express doubt in God's wisdom and love, or ingratitude for all He had done for me. But I had questions that I realized I needed to have answered. My angel told me that it was right that I should ask these questions and that Jesus would be gracious and ready to answer all of them. He promised to arrange a time for me to speak to Jesus in private.

Later I learned that it was, in fact, in Jesus' plan to meet with each of us during this thousand-year period before returning to the earth. The purpose of this time was to answer all such questions to the satisfaction of every being in the universe so that there would be no doubts or misunderstandings in the future.

A few days later, I was escorted to a well-appointed sitting room next to the throne room. As I was directed to be seated, I sank into one of the couches placed around the room. I marveled at the intricate designs of silver and gold thread woven into the blue silk tapestry. Presently Jesus entered the room, attended by several more angels. I rose to greet Him but fell to my knees in worship before Him. As He stepped near, the light that surrounded Him enveloped me in a warm glow. He gently touched my head and bade me rise. We were now seated before a table that looked to be made of a cut and polished ruby crystal set in gold, and an angel brought us each a golden glass of delicious fruit juice.

Jesus leaned forward, looking into my eyes. "You have some questions for me?" He invited. Those eyes! Every time I looked into them, I felt like I was diving into a sea of love. If that sounds weird, I apologize; human language fails me here. Kindness, patience, personal interest - these were all communicated to my soul through those eyes.

"Yes, Lord," I began, "There are several loved ones - souls that I know You laid upon my heart to love, nurture, and pray for - but they are not here. I don't question your wisdom, but I feel the need to understand why." He nodded, encouraging me to continue. I decided to ask about them one by one. I started with you. "It just breaks my heart," the tears instantly welled up in my eyes as memories flooded my mind. I could see a deep sadness, to the point of pain in Jesus' eyes. I realized that this conversation was not going to be easy for Him either. The aching void I felt in my heart for each of my spiritual children and friends was but a faint reflection of the searing pain of loss He felt, not only for those I was inquiring about, but for every human soul who was not here.

Jesus beckoned to an attending angel who brought a very large leather-bound book and laid it upon the table before us. As Jesus opened its pages, scenes from your life began to play out before me. I saw you when you were just a small child, marked by innocence and deeply interested in the stories of Jesus. I saw your guardian angel impressing your mind with the love Jesus had for you. Your little heart was moved to put your childish trust in Him.

On another page, I saw you as a preteen. You were with a group of friends in a place you were not supposed to be. These friends were engaged in sinful pleasures. Your angel urged you to leave their company at once and go to the safety of your parents but you ignored his voice as you were influenced to go along with these "friends" to retain their approval. Later I saw you lie to your parents about the incident to escape punishment. Unfortunately, I saw there were many more instances like this from that time on.

As more pages turned, I saw you in high school. Your parents had chosen to give you a Christian education, and I saw that the godly examples of dedicated teachers and pastors made an impression upon you. As you attended assembly, prayer meetings, and church, the Holy Spirit made special efforts to impress the truths you were hearing upon your heart.

As the next page turned, it glowed with a soft light. The Week of Prayer was in progress. This was the last evening and I heard the speaker make a powerful call at the end of a very moving service. The invitation was to come forward in full surrender to Jesus Christ. I saw the Holy Spirit, like a dove, hovering above you. Your face was alight and as if moved by an unseen hand, you stood to your feet and walked to the front of the church, kneeling at the altar along with several others. I wept for joy as I witnessed your decision to be baptized and give your life in service for the Master.

As the pages turned, the years passed. I saw you graduate from high school. A time when there are so many choices to be made, each one like a portal leading to vastly different futures. You had the opportunity to take a gap year and serve as a student missionary. Some encouraged you to go this direction, and you seemed almost ready to; but your parents, with legitimate concern for your educational opportunities and the need to take advantage of scholarships you were offered, made a strong case for going straight to university. You finally conceded to their judgment, although you still were not certain what course of study you would pursue. Too many decisions! It was bewildering. But as the curtain between the seen and the unseen worlds was pulled aside, I saw the Holy Spirit waiting for you to ask the Lord for direction. He was ready with the answer: "This is the way, walk ye in it." But you were too busy, so caught up in all the plans and logistics and decisions you were being pressed to make, that you forgot to stop and ask. The warning was uttered, "Lean not unto your own understanding," but the admonition went unheeded.

From this point, it was as if I saw two parallel lives being played out before me in the pages of this tome - one, what might have been, and the other as it was. What might have been was a life increasingly dedicated to service with a clear vision of the nearness of Christ's coming and the work that needed to be done for souls. It was a very interesting life with many miracles and adventures; a beautiful and happy union with a soulmate, and the addition of precious children that grew in their love for the Lord. Never did you lack the things necessary for life and happiness, although the income was modest and the living quarters simple.

Sadly the life that was took a much different course with the emphasis placed on worldly wealth, honor, and achievements. You were attracted to a mate who was much more concerned with the commendation of men than of God. Your heart was steadily drawn away from your first love and your commitment to the Savior. You were successful by the world's standards. A good career, a fine house, time and money for amusement and entertainment. But peace and joy were not there. Disagreement and bitterness crept into your marriage and finally led to an ugly divorce. Instead of causing you to realize your need for Jesus in your life, you chose to harbor bitterness for both your spouse and God. The bitterness grew like a tenacious vine strangling the little spiritual life that remained and forming an impenetrable barrier between God's Spirit and your conscience. Never again did you seek after God, nor hear His gentle pleadings.

The book was closed. How incredibly sad I was. How I longed for what might have been. There were no more questions to be asked. "I understand," I said sorrowfully. "But what about the others?"

IV.

Who is Your God?

No one can serve two masters...
Choose for yourselves this day whom you will serve...
But as for me and my house, we will serve the Lord.
Matthew 6:24 & Joshua 24:15

Jesus rose from the couch, and reaching out, took my hand in His. "Come," He spoke in that rich musical bass, "Before we talk about them, let's take a walk. We mustn't look too long on those things that may be discouraging without taking some time to contemplate those things which are right, pure, and beautiful."

We exited the meeting chamber onto the main street of the Crystal City and proceeded to the east gate, just Jesus and I. Incredible gratitude and peace welled up within my being. Like an admiring child, I looked up into the beautiful face of my Hero. He still held my hand in His as we walked along the street made of transparent gold. It occurred to me that He was indeed my exceeding great reward. Even if I had no one else, I would still feel complete in His presence. We walked along in pleasant silence for some time, waving at others as we passed.

We saw that Mary Magdalene had found Matthew and Peter. The three were catching up with each other, sharing memories of their time together with Jesus. I still had not met all the saints I had read so much about. I knew I would have no problem staying occupied for eternity! There were so many people to meet and so many things to learn and do!

My Favorite Bible Hero

Presently, we left the city and were now strolling along a gravel path. The gravel, however, was not gray rocks, but was composed of jewels and gems of many colors. I've always loved collecting beautiful stones and stooped to collect a particularly beautiful one here and there. Jesus smiled at my innocent pleasure in His creation. Shortly, my hands were so full, I realized my collection was going to become impractical. I tossed the beautiful stones back into the path, laughing at the thought that I only had to walk down this path any time I pleased to enjoy these gems again.

The winding path led through stately trees. I would call it a wood, but it was more like a well-manicured park or botanical garden, bright and fragrant with the perfume of many flowers. A gentle breeze rustled the shimmering leaves sending prismatic colors dancing everywhere. Presently, we came to a small arbor with an exquisite little garden bench beneath. I saw a man resting here enjoying the breeze and watching the birds and other small animals that played in the foliage.

"Greetings, Joseph," Jesus called out. "Let me introduce you to my friend." As he rose to greet me, I suddenly realized, this was THE Joseph - Jacob's favorite son. Joseph was always my favorite Bible character - so handsome, so loyal and steadfast in his faith, so kind and forgiving of his brothers! And here he was before me! We three sat down to visit.

At length I began to ask questions I had wondered about for years. "Joseph, how did you find the strength to stand so decidedly for the right when you were taken from your father and home at such a young age? Did you not think maybe God had forsaken you? Were you never tempted to give up your faith in Him?"

He took a deep breath, a faraway look in his smiling eyes. "I did despair for a time. I still remember that lonesome journey to Egypt. I cried bitterly. I was a bit spoiled and used to always being pampered and cared for, and here I was on my own with no one to lean upon for spiritual strength at only 17. I was tempted to give up all trust in God. But at some point on that journey the God of my fathers brought to my mind the many stories my Grandfather Isaac had told me - stories of God's faithfulness - and I determined right there to always be true to God no matter what may come. That day my father's God became MY God."

"I've always marveled at how, no matter what situation you found yourself in, you always rose to the top in favor and responsibility. It's as though you had the 'Midas' touch!'" I smiled. "In Potifar's house, even in the dungeon! How did you do that?"

"I'm not sure what the 'Midas' touch' is..." Joseph looked puzzled.

"Oh! I'm sorry! Of course you wouldn't. You lived long before the Greek civilization. It's a figure of speech referring to how everything this guy,

39

Midas, touched turned to gold." We all laughed at the disconnect that living thousands of years apart sometimes caused in conversations.

"Well, to answer your question, of course God blessed me. But I would say it was because I had learned at a young age to consult duty rather than inclination." Joseph explained. "In everything, I did my duty rather than what I felt like doing. Many times I felt like giving up or getting even with those who wronged me, but always before me was my Grandfather's example of faith and obedience, and how God honored him. I chose to trust my fate to God instead of fretting myself out of His hands."

We had a wonderful conversation together, and I was greatly blessed to see and talk with one of my greatest heroes of faith.

Mark

After returning from our walk, Jesus and I were again seated in the meeting room. The angel had placed a new book upon the table between us.

As Jesus turned the pages of this book I could see Mark first as an adorable little boy, later a gangly teen. There were high points in his Christian experience and then there were very low ones that made me cry. As he grew to manhood, Mark kept walking the fence, trying to keep the pleasures of this world while at the same time maintaining the facade of a good Christian working for the Lord. He had a sincere desire for righteousness. I saw the Holy Spirit plant seeds of faith in his heart and they grew very heartily for some time. But the choice to continue in known sin is fatal to spiritual life.

As the pages of the book turned I saw that over and over he resisted the call of the Holy Spirit to surrender completely, until finally there was no spiritual life remaining. The Holy Spirit was grieved away, never to return.

Jesus looked up, a tear sliding down his cheek. "Without the influence of the Spirit, the human heart is desperately wicked and capable of unthinkable crimes." I squeezed my eyes shut tight, fearing what was coming next. "Mark became totally captive to his base impulses and in the end, he was satisfying his desires at the expense of the innocence and happiness of others, all the while justifying his behavior to himself." I shuddered with horror, my heart breaking for this young man who had held so much promise, as well as for the young lives he had so deeply wounded.

"My children, Why, O why will you die?! You had only to choose life and it would have been yours - happiness, fulfillment, lasting pleasure ..." I was weeping into my hands. "I know, that's how

I feel too," Jesus whispered.

Rachel

Finally wiping my eyes, I asked, "What about Rachel, Lord? She seemed so dedicated to You." Jesus' eyes clouded as He answered "She was, indeed. She had but one fault."

"Only one fault, Lord?" I asked.

"Yes, she thought too highly of her own opinions and, trusting her own understanding, she often refused to listen to the counsel of those with more experience."

"But how could this one fault keep her out of heaven?!" I asked in shocked surprise.

"One thing leads to another, and even a small deviance at the first can leave you far afield in the end. Pride of opinion is a form of idolatry. Putting trust in herself above all else led to distrust of God, and finally, disobedience and direct opposition to God. In the end, Rachel was on the side of those turning over friends and fellow church members to the authorities, thinking she was doing God's service."

"No," I groaned, "not Rachel! How, oh how could she become so misguided and deceived!"

My head was reeling. Salvation was free; Grace was plentiful; full provision had been made for the redemption of every soul. The only condition was surrender. But for so, so many, surrender was judged too high a price to be paid.

"What about Kelly?" I asked. I had lost all contact with her, and I never had any assurance that she had fully given her life to the Lord. I had hoped, though, and prayed a great deal.

"Let us first take some nourishment before we look at any more." Jesus beckoned to one of the angels, asking him to set a place for me at the dining table. We rose and Jesus and the angels escorted me into the dining room adjoining the throne room. Enoch, Moses, Elijah, John the Baptist, and others who were the first fruits of Jesus' resurrection were seated around the elegantly laid table. I was amazed that I would be joining Jesus and this preeminent group for a meal! Who was I to be granted such a privilege!

Again, Jesus served His guests with the assistance of the attending angels. We had an amazing conversation around the table. These great men of God were real people. They shared stories of their experiences while on earth - amazing miracles and even some very humorous incidents. Jesus and the angels joined in the innocent mirth as well. The laughter was healing to the soul.

V.

Tears in Heaven

*"How can I give you up?
As I live," says the Lord GOD, "I have no pleasure in the death
of the wicked; but that the wicked turn from his way and live.
Turn, turn from your evil ways! For why should you die?"
Hosea 11:8 & Ezekiel 33:11*

When the meal was done, Jesus indicated that He was ready to continue working through my questions. It occurred to me that He had spent His whole day, so far, with me.

"Lord, I'm only one among millions of your people who I'm sure all have their own questions to ask You. I hate to take more of Your time." But Jesus just smiled as He led me back to the chamber. "They will each have their questions answered. I have as much time as it takes to give a satisfactory answer to everyone's questions."

Kelly

"Well then, I would like to know what happened to Kelly," I said as I sank into the soft blue couch once more.

"Ah, Kelly." Jesus' eyes softened with a wistful sadness. "Kelly was a very wounded soul. But no wound is so deep that I cannot heal it - if only I am allowed to touch it and make it whole. I never lost a case that was entrusted to me. But, there is nothing I can do if the patient does not trust my remedy.

"Many, like Kelly, refused the remedy and instead insisted on treating their woundedness with the medications of the world - drugs, sex, movies, food, drink, music - whatever can offer a momentary escape from their pain. But these things only numb the pain and hide the sores. They do not heal."

I saw that Kelly had made feeble attempts at following Christ. Like the stony ground hearers in the parable of the sower, spiritual life would spring up in response to an emotional appeal fueled by the enthusiasm of those around her; then as quickly die away when the feeling wore off, or she was not with others who were spiritually strong. She had no root in herself. Her experience was as fleeting as the feelings that prompted it. In the end, she was too concerned with pleasing those around her to stand for any convictions.

As I said before, she was very stubborn, which could have become the valuable traits of determination and perseverance. But her determination was only employed in getting what she wanted, never in striving for mastery of self or remaining true to her convictions. I saw, at last, she felt no more the promptings of the Spirit. She was adrift like a small boat in a vast ocean and was finally dashed against the rocks of sinful habits.

My heart ached with grief. Sometimes I think it would be much easier never to love. Then I would not care; I would not hurt... but neither would I experience companionship with God who is love. Jesus felt the pain more keenly than I ever could. He was a man of sorrows and acquainted with grief, and looking into his sorrowing eyes, I understood in a measure what His heart was going through. Then I felt myself enveloped in His embrace, comforting and being comforted.

Gabe
With a ragged sigh, I sank back into the couch. "I have one more I need to know about, if my heart can bear it."

"Gabe..." He spoke the name with a catch in His voice.

"Yes, Lord. You put that young man into our family and our hearts. You know how hard I worked for his salvation, and I thought he was on the right path... I prayed for him every day. I thought You had promised me that You had Him in Your hands and would never let him go." I was shaking with sobs now and could not say more.

"Never did I let him go. It was he that took himself out of my hands. As you know, I will never force myself upon anyone. I did everything I could to draw his heart to Me. I called him to work for Me; I opened doors before him. My Spirit was beside him to guide and direct. But Satan had his alluring devices wherewith to wean the soul's affections from Me and place them upon earthly, sensual things.

"More and more of his time was spent gaming, watching movies, and scrolling through social media. He had no time to spend with Me. No time for communion with nature, with his own soul, and with God. He became blind to eternal things. He was drawn to increasingly crude and debasing material further numbing his conscience.

"I well remember the last time my Spirit pleaded with him. He was again indulging in base and impure entertainment. I called to him, but the ears of his conscience were all but deaf from ignoring Me in the past. Your prayers for him weighed on My heart and amplified My own love for Gabe. After all, I died for him. I carried the guilt for all these sins that were now separating his soul from Me. I could feel the pain of it all over again. And so, because I could not give up on him, I shouted into his conscience, giving him the strongest warning of his peril. For a second it jolted him. Briefly, I arrested his attention. I flashed into his mind a memory of you praying with him about this very temptation.

"He winced, visibly shaken. Then, with a burst of anger, he screamed at Me to leave him alone, telling Me that I was an unwanted intrusion. He shut and barred the door so that he would never be bothered again by My still small voice pleading with him. I left him alone. There was nothing more I could do."

Jesus paused, a faraway expression in his eyes. He seemed to forget I was there. As He continued, I felt as though I was eavesdropping on His conversation with Himself.

"When Gabe was a child, I loved him and called him away from his sins. I taught him how to walk, leading him along by the hand with My kindness and love. I freed him from chains of sin that had bound him. But the more I called him, the farther he moved from Me. Eventually, he didn't even know or care that it was I who took care of him. Oh, how can I give you up? How can I let you go? How can I allow you to be destroyed? My heart is torn within Me, and My compassion overflows. O My son, I died for you so you wouldn't have to die! O, Gabe, My son, My son...." (Hosea 11:1-9 & 2 Samuel 18:33)

Tears were streaming down Jesus' face and He

could speak no more. Great sobs shook his frame. I beheld the sight in amazement. My own heart ached as well, but here was the Son of God, glorified, all-powerful, robed in light and majesty, but still very human. He was no stranger to the emotions I was feeling - indeed, He was the creator of human emotion. His empathy and compassion are infinite; His love for His children, even His lost children, stronger than death.

I could see that He had done everything in his power to answer my prayers for Gabe. His love for him was much stronger than even a mother's. I felt the bitterness of defeat at losing the battle for his soul, but I had not left all heaven to live a life of toil and hardship and then die crushed by the weight of the guilt of Gabe's sins in hopes that he would accept the gift I offered him at such personal cost only to be rejected, yelled at to go away! Jesus had borne all this! How could a human heart, even one as big as His, bear that kind of rejection and defeat?

I never dreamed there would be so many tears in heaven! The Bible says God will wipe away all our tears. Now I realize that is after the millennium, after the earth is made new and the universe is in harmony once again. Yes, God will wipe away our tears, but I wonder ...who will wipe away His?

Jesus finally wiped his eyes and looked at me with a weak smile. "We need to rejoice for the many souls that have been redeemed. Come, you need to meet a few more people."

VI.

Joy in Heaven

*There will be more joy in heaven over one sinner who repents
than over ninety-nine just persons
who need no repentance.
Luke 15:7*

*The Mighty One, will save;
He will rejoice over you with gladness,
He will quiet you with His love,
He will rejoice over you with singing.
Zephaniah 3:17*

Jesus and I left the room and again ventured down the main street of the beautiful city. This time we left through the west gate and emerged into a meadow of living green, bejeweled with a thousand wildflowers in every iridescent hue of the rainbow. In the distance, I could see majestic mountains capped with glittering gemstones instead of snow! Rivulets flowed down their sides and merged into streams and rivers that flowed out through the valley, watering orchards of fruit trees, vineyards with grapes ready for harvest, flowering trees of every color, and all the flora in the meadow.

I breathed in deeply, filling my lungs with the fresh, crisp mountain air. Suddenly seized by a youthful surge of energy, I began to skip and then twirl through the grass, arms stretched out and head thrown back in abandon. The meadow, the mountains, the glistening city whirled past my vision, and suddenly, losing my balance, I tumbled into the soft grass, laughing at myself in half embarrassed mirth.

I could hear Jesus laughing with delight as well, and then another face appeared above me as I lay trying to regain my equilibrium. A tanned face with dancing eyes and a broad smile. He reached out a hand and helped me up.

Matthew & Joel

"Hi mom, I'm home!" He exclaimed with all the glee of a little child, hugging me tightly. I held him at arm's length, not quite believing my eyes!

"Matthew! It really IS you!" His grin broadened further with delight at being able to surprise me so. Then looking around, I saw a lovely young lady, whom I realized now was Matthew's partner, Melissa, holding by the hand a sweet little girl who was the spitting image of her daddy! Next to them was another surprise - Joel.

Standing there with his characteristic dignified bearing, a most becoming crown upon his dark curly head, Joel wore a delighted smile and laughed at my happiness in seeing him.

These two young men were good friends at the

Christian high-school where I had taught. Both were very dear to me. But as I watched the directions they each took in life, I despaired of ever seeing them in heaven. Even still, I never stopped praying for them.

Matt was impulsive by nature and rode an emotional roller coaster. I felt like he had somehow gotten an incorrect view of God's character that had left him not too interested in giving such a being control of his life.

Joel, on the other hand, was very intellectual and very much in possession of himself. He excelled in his studies and became successful in his career. Joel did not feel any need for a savior. He had everything under control. My constant prayer for them both through the years had been, "Lord, do whatever it takes to bring them to their knees at the foot of the cross. Help them see their need of You."

So what had it taken to bring them home? I looked at Jesus with this question in my eyes, and he smiled, nodding his head toward them. We proceeded to walk together through the meadow with Amy, Matt's little girl, flitting around us like a butterfly picking this flower and that, exclaiming in delight over every little discovery.

In answer to my question, Joel replied, "I finally ran up against something in my life that

I totally lacked the resources to deal with. I was literally brought to my knees with the realization that I did need God in my life. I knew where to go to find Him. After all, I had grown up in a good Christian home. I guess it was a lot like the prodigal son's story. I was finally bankrupt and I returned home to my Father."

"For me," Matt said, looking tenderly at his little daughter, "It was becoming a father that brought me to see the love of my Father. Melissa and I had both been raised in Christian homes, but we were not following Christ. I was scared to death of commitment in any relationship. I held back from God, and I held back from marrying Melissa even though we were very much in love." A knowing look passed between them.

"Then, one day we discovered we were going to have a baby. I was pretty scared. I can see now that this was in God's providence, but at the time, I felt like running. I didn't want the responsibility that now rested upon me. I knew I needed to make a commitment to Melissa and get married if we were going to provide a safe home for our child. As you know, I was adopted because my birth mother was in a similar situation and did not have the resources to take responsibility for raising me.

"I determined there was no way I was going to let Melissa and my child be put in that same situation. But I didn't know how I was going to love this new little being. I finally reasoned that I would eventually come to love our baby when it could respond to us, or when it could move around and play, or speak. Basically, I thought a father's love would gradually develop in response to my child's ability and willingness to interact with me.

"I was completely unprepared for the wave of fatherly love that suddenly flooded through my body when I held my newborn daughter for the first time. Nothing had prepared me for this. Where did this love come from? Amy had done nothing to inspire it, or to deserve it. It was just there. I was overwhelmed. And right there God spoke to my soul and said, 'If you, as a human father, can experience such a depth of love for your little one - how much do you think I, your Heavenly Father, love you?'

"As I was thinking about this insight, God spoke again to my mind, 'Wouldn't it break your heart if Amy never responded to your love - never loved you in return?'

"That right there was the turning point for me. I was totally broken by the realization that I had not responded to God's constant, unconditional love for me.

"Melissa and I got married and we started attending church again and taking our relationship with God seriously. Little by little, God drew our hearts to Him in love and obedience, and because of His patient love and grace, we are here today!"

Tears of happiness welled up in my eyes as I realized how incredibly God had answered my prayers. I looked at Jesus, and in the unspoken communication between us, I sensed the thrill and the privilege of working together with Him and enjoying the reward of our labor of love together.

VII.

Ransomed

Why should I fear in the days of evil?
Those who trust in their wealth
And boast in the multitude of their riches,
None of them can by any means redeem his brother,
Nor give to God a ransom for him—
For the redemption of their souls is costly... Psalm 5-8
[The Lord] gave Himself a ransom for all. 1 Timothy 2:6

"I will ransom them from the power of the grave; I will redeem them from death." Hosea 13:14
And the ransomed of the Lord shall return, And come to Zion with singing, With everlasting joy on their heads.
Isaiah 35:10

The days and years passed in continual wonder and delight as we all enjoyed fellowship together in this place of perfect harmony and love. My husband and I enjoyed many long walks through the beautiful garden of Eden, and often groups of friends and relatives would join us and our sons for exploration expeditions into the mountains to the west. On one such occasion, I got the long-awaited opportunity to hear Ari's story. The others in our hiking party were forging ahead as Ari and I fell behind talking and stopping frequently to inspect a new flower here, a little bird there.

Ari's Story

"Ari, tell me what happened in the final days on earth. Last I knew, you had quite lost your focus on spiritual things, and were enjoying a pretty comfortable life as business was doing quite well for you."

"Yes, mom, I was making good money. I was getting rich!" He laughed somewhat ruefully. "But, somehow, I never felt satisfied. I had no peace. This thought kept nagging me, I think you told me this once, 'What good does it do a man if he gains the whole world, but loses his own soul in the end.' God had called me to work for Him - you knew that, mom."

"Yes, son. I remember that calling was like fire in your bones. It was a passion I had never seen in you before. But you ran into obstacles trying to follow God's call. I prayed you would be patient and wait on God to open the way before you."

"My dad really wanted me to go into business with him. He thought my idea, my desire to work for God, was foolish and impractical. So, I eventually just gave in and went along. I think something inside me died with my dream. I drifted further and further away from God as my time was absorbed with worldly pursuits."

"So what happened?!" I asked, anxious to hear the whole story. Ari's eyes sparkled with pleasure at my suspense as though savoring the exciting memories he was about to share.

"I got kidnapped!"

"Kidnapped?! What do you mean? What happened? Don't keep me in such suspense, Ari!" I exclaimed, impatiently grabbing his arm.

"So, I had to go out of the country on business. The city was close to an area where there was a lot of political unrest. I didn't think it was going to be a problem for me. I was going to be in the 'safe' district that was under the control of the government. But... wouldn't you know it, my taxi driver got lost taking me to my hotel, and we got into the bad area of town.

"Suddenly several rebel soldiers with machine guns blocked the road, jumped into the taxi, and took it over at gunpoint. They hand-cuffed both me and the taxi driver and took off with us for their compound some distance out in the hills. I guess they thought I would be a valuable hostage and they could use me to get a nice ransom. They took my luggage, and made me strip down to my undies with an AK-47 to my head! They took my nice suit and shoes, my expensive watch, searched my briefcase, and took a bit of cash I had. I was pretty upset and scared. I thought I was going to die right there.

"It hit me that I was not ready to die. I realized

I had thought I was on the path to the good life - gaining the world, you know - but now it was worth nothing to me because if I died right then, I would be lost. I felt that lostness, that emptiness, right in the middle of my chest.

"I prayed... for the first time in a long time! 'God, I don't want to die! You called me to do something for You, and I haven't followed You. I gave up on You! Forgive me, Lord! If you can still use me now please work through me even in this situation.' You know, I don't think I had ever given myself completely to God before. I always kept part ownership! That was my problem all along when I couldn't live the way I thought a Christian should. It was discouraging, and I kinda gave up, I guess.

"But after praying that prayer, I felt totally at peace for the first time... but I felt excited too! Remember, I always wanted to do something dangerous for God... maybe die preaching the gospel to savages. Well, I got my wish!!"

"They killed you?"

"Not right then! I had to preach the gospel first!" Ari laughed.

It was hard to hear each other now as we had reached the base of a beautiful waterfall. Its roar drowned out Ari's laugh as the water cascaded down the verdant slope and fell gracefully into the pool before us, the spray blowing from its froth reminiscent of a bridal veil. We rested a moment and quenched our thirst from the clear water.

"How did you get the opportunity to preach the gospel to your captors?" I asked as we proceeded up the trail again.

"There was another guy in the camp, a Filipino man. They had captured him several days before. Now, this guy was a real Christian. He had somehow managed to keep a small Bible. I guess it wasn't anything the rebels wanted, so they let him keep it. We started reading that little Bible together. I got so excited. I couldn't believe I had missed all those beautiful messages!

"I told this guy I wanted to preach!" Ari laughed, "It was like fire in my bones. So I did! I stood up and started telling these guys about Jesus; that He died for them to pay the ransom Satan demanded for their lives! These guys were drunk and high on drugs, and they just looked at me like I was crazy. But I kept it up. There was one big, mean guy that kept trying to make me shut up, but several others wanted to hear more. They would ask me to tell them more when the big guy wasn't around. Several of them accepted Jesus as their Savior! They wanted to be baptized, so my friend and I studied with them as much as we could."

"So what happened to them? Were you finally rescued?" I asked, anxious to hear the conclusion.

"One night, while it was very dark, the army found the guerrilla hideout, and there was a lot of fighting back and forth. I don't know if they were trying to rescue us, if they knew we were there, or what. I think I was shot - by which side, I don't know. But the next thing I knew, I heard an incredibly loud trumpet blast, and I looked up and saw this cloud of angels! Then, I realized I was in the first resurrection! I was laughing and crying all at the same time!

"By the way, three of the guys we were studying with are HERE! See these stars right here?" Ari took his crown from his head with a flourish and pointed to three sparkling jewels on one side. "These stars are for them! I have stars in my crown! Look, mom, look at all these stars! I don't even know yet who they're all for!"

I wiped tears of joy from my eyes as I laughed. Ari was so animated. Suddenly we both burst forth with a song of praise to our great Redeemer. Our voices echoed and re-echoed from one hill to the next. We heard answering voices ahead on the trail as the rest of our group joined in the song, filling the entire valley with the harmonies and swelling to a mighty anthem like the voice of many waters. "Holy, Holy, Holy is the Lord…"

Meeting More Friends

Over the years I got to know so many wonderful people. Developing deeper relationships is so painless when you realize that they will never be interrupted by distance, death, or disagreement. How wonderful the thought!

We got to know our angel friends more intimately and spent many enjoyable hours conversing with them about the history of heaven and what it was like before the earth was created. Discussions of Lucifer's rebellion, however, still caused them noticeable pain. To us, Lucifer, or Satan, as we all called him now, was an impersonal enemy we could not relate to. But to these angels, he had been a much-loved leader, friend, and confidant.

Some of them recounted conversations they'd had with Lucifer, and the crafty arguments he had used to deceive them into distrusting God's government. It sounded as intriguing as any earthly political propaganda campaign. We recognized these same tactics used in the final movements on earth that brought about the death decree for those who would not worship the beast.

Several angels told how they were for a while convinced that Lucifer was right, and actually aided him in his rebellion before becoming aware that they were being deceived and led astray. They shuddered to think of how close they had come to eternal misery and ruin. We all realized that it was only by the grace of God that any of us had escaped the wiles of this master deceiver!

VIII.
Healing Our Brokenness

*He was wounded for our transgressions,
He was bruised for our iniquities; The chastisement for our
peace was upon Him, And by His stripes
we are healed.
Isaiah 53:5*

*He heals the brokenhearted And binds up their wounds.
Psalm 147:3*

One day I was walking along my favorite garden path with Scott, my second-born son. It was so wonderful to have the time to just be together enjoying this beautiful place.

"Mother, do you remember what a struggle I had -- and a lot of my friends had -- with negative self-talk back when I was growing up? It kept so many of us from fully realizing and accepting how much God loved us. I think it was probably one of Satan's most successful ploys to trap God's children in the darkness of despair and then pull them into all kinds of destructive habits."

"Yes, I do remember," I replied, shaking my head as I recalled the difficulty of counteracting these negative thoughts. "So many people could not believe that they could be loved. They might even believe that God is love and that God loves everyone ... everyone else, that is, but not them, personally. Because God knows everything, right? And since He knows everything, that meant He knew how bad you really were. He knew what everyone else only suspected. So, sure, He loved everyone else, but not you!"

"Right! And until I actually grasped the fact that God loved me PERSONALLY ... UNCONDITIONALLY ... no matter what I might have done, there was no possibility of my gaining freedom from sin. Sin is literally a symptom of not seeing your value in Christ, of being alone. If you don't believe anyone could love you unconditionally, then you are on your own and have to look out for yourself - and that's selfishness, the root of all sin."

"You know, I was just talking with your grandfather about that very thing." I smiled as I recalled finding my father deep in the historical archives vault. It was his favorite place to be. He always did love history and research.

"I hadn't had a chance to visit with him much before. We got to talking about his life on earth and how he was never shown the love of a father. He never saw an example of a loving relationship between his parents, and he couldn't recall his father ever saying, 'I love you, son', or 'I'm proud of you.' As you might imagine, this left a huge void in his heart and an inability to feel love from anyone - or for anyone. Oh, he was a good dad. I believe God supplied his lack and helped him demonstrate and verbalize love for me. He understood love in an intellectual way, but he never felt loved by his Heavenly Father."

"That's so sad! How did he come to know God's grace and redeeming love for him, then?"

"He never really grasped that love until the resurrection! He was weeping as he told me how incredible it was to actually FEEL that love for the first time. It literally filled his heart and healed that lifelong wound.

"He's here by the grace of God. God knows our frailty, our background, how our minds work. He understands and accepts us for who we are in Christ Jesus. Grandpa intellectually grasped the truth about who God is. He clung to that by faith even if he never felt it."

"Wow! But to finally realize the fullness of God's love… what an amazing, healing experience!"

As we rounded a bend in the trail, we saw two ladies walking together ahead. We called out in greeting, and as they turned to acknowledge us, We saw that it was Mary Magdalene and Deanna, a former schoolmate of Scott's!

Deanna & Mary Magdalene

"Come join us," Deanna called out.

We had hardly caught up when she reached out to embrace us, her eyes alight with love and peace, her smile beaming from perfect contentment. Nothing was hiding behind that smile. On earth, she had always worn a smile, at least around me. She had looked like everything was okay; but if you had looked deep enough into her hazel eyes, you could have seen that there was pain, fear, even hopelessness there. She had been careful to wear long sleeves so no one could see the scars that were but a faint hint of the agony she felt inside. But now she was yet another testament to the power of Jesus' healing love.

"I was just telling Deanna about the first time I met Jesus," Mary smiled, inviting us to join their conversation.

"Oh, do continue," I urged, "I've been anxious to hear your testimony myself!"

"Well, I was telling Deanna how my parents died when I was quite young and my older brother and sister ended up raising me. I had a lot of trauma from the loss, and even though my dear sister did her best to raise me, I somehow didn't feel loved. Then my uncle started abusing me. I felt so worthless. He told me as much. I felt so much shame, I ended up running away, and then, to make a living I became a prostitute. ... My life just spiraled out of control. Demons started tormenting me, driving me to do things I didn't want to do. I turned to strong drink to dull my pain, I would even cut myself to somehow give release to all the pain I felt inside.

"One day I was propositioned by one of the Pharisees. Yes! --You wouldn't expect that, would you? It wasn't the first time. I no longer had any respect for myself - no dignity. I figured this was the only thing I was good for.

"I didn't realize that this was a setup. All of a sudden several men barged in and dragged me down the street, right into the temple courtyard! I was dropped unceremoniously in front of Jesus, the new teacher from Galilee! I was terrified. A delegation of priests and Pharisees were asking Him if they should stone me to death! Jesus said whoever was sinless could start throwing stones and I braced myself for the inevitable. I knew some of these men were not sinless, but they might think they were, and surely others were. But ... nothing happened! Slowly, one by one, all those priests and Pharisees slunk away!

"When it was just Jesus there, He spoke to me, 'Has no one condemned you?' I had never had a man speak to me like that before... what I mean is .... He spoke to me as though I had value

... not condescendingly, not like I was just a piece of trash, but like I was a real person! I still cannot put into words the feelings that welled up within me. I looked tentatively into his kind eyes and said, 'No man, Lord.' I really didn't know what to expect next. He smiled tenderly, looking deep into my soul. I felt that He could read all the sordid history of my life of sin. But instead of feeling disdain and condemnation under his gaze, I felt enveloped in love. He said, 'Neither do I condemn you. Go and sin no more.'

"I didn't want to move! I felt safe near Jesus. For once in my life, I thought I might actually be able to live a respectable life as long as I never left His side. Just to know that someone valued me, loved me, cared about me ... I felt forgiven for the first time."

Tears welled up in Deanna's eyes. "That's how I felt the first time I met Jesus," she exclaimed. "Of course, I couldn't see Him in person, but I felt the same overwhelming love when the Holy Spirit revealed to my darkened mind just who Jesus was and how much He loved me and wanted to save me! Of course, it wasn't a 'happily ever after' scenario. I struggled with old habits and negative self-talk, but every time I came back to the foot of the cross and 'looked' at Jesus, I found the strength again to go forward."

"Absolutely," Mary agreed. "I fell back into sin over and over again - seven times in fact! I can't believe how patient Jesus was with me. He was always there to pick me up again, to forgive me, love me, and set my feet again on the right path." Mary shook her head in amazement, remembering. "That's why I love Him so much," she concluded reverently.

At that moment we rounded a curve in the trail and there on the left was the most beautiful little butterfly garden I had ever seen. Mary and Deanna both exclaimed in delight at how well the flowers were attracting the butterflies. Asters, phlox, salvia, and many other flowers in full bloom sent their fragrance into the gentle breeze. Many varieties of butterflies flitted among the flowers, sipping sweet nectar from this one and that.

"This has been our project," Deanna beamed, "Mary and I have been working on landscaping this little garden for quite some time."

"And just look at all the different butterflies that have found our little spot!" Mary gasped as a particularly gorgeous Ulysses butterfly with iridescent blue wings landed on her shoulder.

Scott sat down on a moss covered rock beside the little stream that gurgled and babbled its way through the little garden. "This is absolutely beautiful, ladies! What would you think if Matt and I built a little bench for your garden? The latest design we came up with would look perfect beneath this maple tree."

Mary was delighted with the offer. I suggested making a little reflecting pool between the shade tree and the flower beds and putting some colorful fish in it. We gained so much enjoyment from the many things we had been able to create and the skills that we had developed over the years with instruction and encouragement from our angel friends. God, the creator and lover of beauty placed within every one of us a measure of creativity, a love of beauty and the desire and ability to learn and develop new skills. These pursuits brought us such joy and fulfillment and endless hours of pleasure as we now enjoyed unlimited time to devote to their improvement.

Our conversation continued in this vein as we walked along together for quite a while. A lot of healing of the heart and mind was taking place during this thousand year period. Many of God's children, though they trusted God completely and loved Him with everything they had, still had hurts, scars of the heart, and misunderstandings that needed to be remedied. We were told that the leaves of the tree of life were for the healing of the nations. Angels spent many hours mentoring these individuals, often over a glass of Fresca made with leaves from the tree of life!

I always thought Jesus would just transform our minds the instant we were glorified and we would have perfect wholeness in the way our minds functioned. But now I realize with what respect God honors our free will and the individuality with which He created us. Because of this,

He reasons with us and brings our minds into harmony with His according to the natural laws of the mind. This takes time, but I was observing the beauty and reward of this healing process.

IX.
Before the Throne

*I looked, and behold,
a great multitude which no one could number,
of all nations, tribes, peoples, and tongues,
standing before the throne and before the Lamb,
clothed with white robes, with palm branches in their hands,
and crying out with a loud voice, saying,
"Salvation belongs to our God who sits on the throne,
and to the Lamb!"
All the angels stood around the throne
and the elders and the four living creatures, and fell on their
faces before the throne and worshiped God, saying:
"Amen! Blessing and glory and wisdom,
Thanksgiving and honor and power and might,
Be to our God forever and ever. Amen."
Revelation 7:9-12*

Time was flying by! In one sense it felt like we had just arrived, while in another it seemed we had always been here. Earth seemed a very distant memory. Harmony and unity of spirit had grown among all of God's children so that intertwining ties of friendship and companionship bound us all together in an unbroken family.

The science of salvation proved to be an unending source of mind-blowing discoveries, and our awe and love for our Redeemer grew as our understanding of His love deepened. The incredible beauty of God's character continually amazed me.

I think the most amazing aspect of His method of governing the universe was demonstrated to me by His complete transparency. I first experienced this through Jesus' willingness to show me just what He had done in the lives of each person I had prayed for. He showed that He had done everything in His power to win their hearts and He revealed to me their choices, which He has bound Himself to respect. He would never force someone to follow Him. The foundation of His government is love, and love alone can awaken love. No hidden agenda or manipulation tactics were ever employed in His attempts to save - only a loving appeal to the head and the heart.

Now, there was but one task remaining before the culmination of the Great Controversy - the judgment of the wicked.

Worship Before the Throne

The hour of worship was always the highlight of our day, and today was no different. Every member of the heavenly family came together before the throne of God; the angels flew in from all directions from their assignments; friends and families clustered together in happy little knots as they made their way to the sea of glass. As we emerged onto this vast expanse, we each took our places and awaited the signal from Gabriel to begin the opening song of praise.

I marveled anew at the grandeur of this place! Because of Jesus' sacrifice, we were given the privilege of coming boldly into this place by faith to ask for the things we had need of, yet how little we realized or valued this tremendous privilege! What a faint perception we had of what it meant to come before the throne of God! This great throne was set high above the crystal sea. Wide golden steps led up to the flaming throne and a river of fire poured forth from under the throne and flowed like molten lava down the center of the steps. Huge jasper and sardonyx stones that looked as though they were on fire themselves, bordered the cascade as it plunged over the last terrace and flowed out beneath the surface of the sea of glass. Beyond the sea, it emerged as the river of life flowing through the Garden of Eden.

Today as the hour of worship concluded, Jesus stepped down from his place on the throne to make an important announcement. The entire congregation fell silent as He spoke. "The Court of the Universe will convene tomorrow. As you know, the cases of the wicked must be brought before the court for each sentence to be ratified. All heavenly beings are called to assemble on the sea of glass at the appointed time."

The Judgment of the Wicked

As we all filed out to attend to our varied pursuits, a group of us discussed the implications of this important event we would be involved with the next day.

"What an amazing God we have!" My husband observed. "He knows all things. He could just as easily pass sentence upon all the wicked without consulting us, yet in His wisdom, he lays everything open to the universe so that there will never be any question about His justice."

My husband and first-born son, Tony, had joined my father in spending a lot of time in the vault researching earth's history and the plan of salvation wrought out through the ages in God's wisdom.

"So what will our responsibility be as part of the court proceedings?" I was concerned about having to pass sentence upon loved ones who were not here.

My father repeated 1 Corinthians 6:2 - "Do you not know that the saints will judge the world?"

"I almost wish God would just do the judging and I'll just trust that He knows best!" I sighed. "But wait, didn't Jesus say, 'the Father judges no one, but has committed all judgment to the Son?'"

"Yes, He did say that in John 5:22, but it's interesting that in John 12:47-48 He says, "And if anyone hears My words and does not believe, I do not judge him; the word that I have spoken will judge him in the last day." Tony pointed out.

"So how does that actually work?" I asked a bit confused.

We stood pondering these questions for a moment when we noticed a couple of our angel friends had been listening with interest to our conversation. Turning to them, we asked if they could enlighten us.

My guardian angel answered with a question, "when you plant a kernel of wheat in the ground, what grows?"

"Well, wheat, of course," we all chorused.

"This is a law of the universe. Whatever you plant, that's what you will reap in the end. Living by the law of love produces a life of obedience and brings life. Likewise, living for oneself apart from God results in death because God is the source of all life and without Him, no one can live."

"In the judgment of the wicked," another angel added, "each life will be examined, comparing the deeds recorded in the books of record with the law of love and liberty to see if they match. The names written in the book of death are those people who rejected Christ's sacrifice for them. It must be seen if the deeds they have sown in their lifetimes could produce life without Christ. God has said the wages - the results or consequences - of sin is death, but Satan claims this is not true. The universe must judge who is right."

Deanna's eyes widened, "You mean, this judgment isn't only determining the fate of the wicked, it's also proving whether God is true and just!"

"That's true," my guardian angel continued, "God has chosen to allow the entire universe to judge Him as well! If everyone is not convinced that His ways are just and righteous, there would be a chance that sin could rise up again."

"Wow! That makes sense. I think I'm starting to understand. But tell me, how are the sentences for the wicked to be determined?" I was still concerned with the idea that I might have to assign some kind of sentence to a lost loved one.

"The further out of harmony with the law of love their lives were, the longer and greater their suffering will be as they come into God's presence after the millennium." He explained. "This is the sentence they have brought upon themselves, and this is what the heavenly hosts must ratify as we judge each case."

We each had a lot to think about as we resumed our activities for the day. I knew this task of judgment was going to be a long and difficult one for me.

X.
The Court of the Universe

*And I saw thrones, and they sat on them,
and judgment was committed to them.
And they lived and reigned with Christ for a thousand years.
Then I saw a great white throne and Him who sat on it,
from whose face the earth and the heaven fled away.
And there was found no place for them. And I saw the dead,
small and great, standing before God, and books were opened.
And another book was opened, which is the Book of Life.
And the dead were judged according to their works,
by the things which were written in the books.
Revelation 20:4, 11-12*

At the appointed judgment hour, I quietly found my seat in the section designated for the 144,000. Just in front of us were twenty-four small thrones set in a semicircle facing the great throne. My eyes swept upward, taking in the massive golden steps ascending the terraces and at the top, the brilliant, fiery white throne.

My son drew my attention back with a tap on my arm. I looked to the right and saw that the twenty-four elders were now entering, dressed in brilliant white robes, golden crowns on their heads. They took their seats upon the twenty-four thrones. After several moments, the angel, Gabriel, gave a long blast of the trumpet and we all stood at attention with eyes fixed on the curtain of light that shimmered with the brilliance of a thousand prisms behind the fiery throne.

The Ancient of Days entered, attended by four Seraphim. He took His seat upon the throne, His brilliant white robes of light filling the temple. I could see His snow white hair beneath a crown that gleamed with the brilliance of the sun; His face and arms shone like polished gemstones. The Seraphim reverently covered their faces with one set of wings, while another pair covered their bodies and with the third pair, they flew, hovering around the throne.

These four magnificent beings began a fugue, quietly at first with two chanting, "Holy, Holy, Holy, Lord God Almighty!" While the others echoed in response, "Past, present, and future!" The voices swelled and crescendoed until the very arches and pillars of the temple trembled. The sound of thunder rolled from the fiery brilliance of the throne. A rainbow of glowing emerald light emanated from the throne and surrounded it completely.

Jesus now entered and sat on the right hand of God. A rushing wind swept through the assembly, blowing my hair back from my face as the Spirit of God made its entrance appearing as seven swirling flames of fire before the throne. Smoke filled the temple until nothing was visible. The throng of attendants bowed in reverent awe as the twenty-four elders knelt before the Godhead and cast their crowns before the throne.

As the smoke subsided in the now hushed courtroom, we rose and beheld several angels bringing in record books which they opened before the whole assembly. Upon them was written the name of each person who had not relied upon the merits of Jesus. Below each name was written their wicked deeds as though etched in letters of fire. No blood covered their sins. They had not confessed them, nor felt their need of the pardoning blood of Christ.

Each name was read before the court along with the sins they had committed. After each reading, the Father asked the Son if His blood had not covered these sins. "No," was His sad reply, "I do not know them; they did not accept the sacrifice offered for their sins." Then, the Father would ask the recording angel to read the sentence marked against the name after which the entire assembly would say, "Amen! Great and marvelous are your works, O Lord God, Almighty. Just and true are your judgments, O King of all the nations."

Even the fallen angels and Lucifer himself were sentenced according to their works. Satan's sentence was horrific as the responsibility for all the sins he had tempted the righteous to commit came back upon himself. The judgment was a solemn and unpleasant task for us to be a part of; however, because of this process we each realized beyond a shadow of a doubt that these individuals had chosen their destiny by their own free will despite God's freely offered grace and mercy. By not requesting the mediation of the Son of God and accepting His sacrifice, there was no blood to cover their sins; and by so choosing, they had entered a guilty plea to the court of heaven. They had willingly chosen death and rejected life.

Although I saw and understood this, it did not make it any easier when Mark's name was read, or Kelly's, or Gabe's, or any of the others. The sentences read were not arbitrary pronouncements from the Deity, but were rather acknowledgments of what each had chosen by his own course of action. How heartrending, I thought. Would each of these individuals have chosen to cling to their sins if they could have seen this moment; could have heard what I was hearing now, and seen the pain that their decisions caused the Son of God, their guardian angel, their loved ones? And yet, they were each told very plainly that the wages of sin would be death, but that the gift of God was eternal life to all who would believe… but they didn't believe it. I shook my head in amazement.

The judgment process took many days, there were so many names written in the book of death. At what an incredible cost this experiment with sin had been conducted. But in God's infinite wisdom He knew that only by allowing it to run its course could the universe be forever inoculated against its recurrence.

Preparing for the Big Move

All heaven was astir. The judgment had finally exhausted the book of death and all the righteous universe was satisfied that God had judged righteously and had successfully maintained the foundation of His government in love. The thousand years were nearly completed and a feeling of excitement filled the air as preparations were being made. Every angel and every person was busy completing their tasks like a well ordered army. Heaven was preparing for the big move!

My mother and I had been working on making curtains for the windows in my mansion and I was finishing up a mural I was painting on one wall. Ari, Scott, and Tony were planning how they would explore the new earth and map it out. Mother hoped to build a small cottage next to a quiet mountain lake and plant a good sized vegetable garden. We each had so many exciting plans and ideas for when we got settled in our new home.

But a recurring thought kept coming to me which sent a throb of pain through my heart each time. Before that new earth could be created, sin must be dealt with once and for all. We would see the lost again. They would be raised in the second resurrection. Would I see Gabe or Rachel? Would I see you? I couldn't imagine how I would feel about that. I wondered too, what would the earth look like after so long with no one living there. Would I recognize anything?

XI.
The End of a Thousand Years

*Then I saw an angel coming down from heaven,
having the key to the bottomless pit and a great chain in his
hand. He laid hold of the dragon, that serpent of old, who is
the Devil and Satan, and bound him for a thousand years;
and he cast him into the bottomless pit, and shut him up,
and set a seal on him, so that he should deceive the nations
no more till the thousand years were finished.
But after these things he must be released for a little while.
Revelation 20:1-3*

As the last grains of time fell through the cosmic hourglass, the thousand years came to an end. Jesus again stood at the head of the millions and billions of the heavenly family, this time ushering us out through the city gates. Surrounded by myriads of angels, we looked like an enormous, brilliant cloud as we passed through the portals of Orion and out into the vastness of space. The beauty of the stars and galaxies surrounding us took our breath away! After some time, we passed through the Orion Arm, one of the spiral arms of the Milky Way with clusters of starts, some brilliantly blue, others rich and red. We passed on into the emptiness of space. Finally we could recognize our little solar system. Closer and closer we came to the little planet we called Earth. That one little speck in the vast universe that had been the theater for unfallen beings to witness the outcome of Satan's claims against God. Now the final showdown was about to take place.

As we drew near enough to see the earth's surface, it appeared formless and empty. A heavy acrid fog hung over large expanses of barren wasteland. Ice covered much of its broken surface which was marred by huge craters left by the impact of meteors. Large areas were covered by lava long since cooled to form a crusty, jagged expanse as hard as iron. Nothing about this planet looked hospitable. It bore no resemblance to the place I had called home so long ago.

As the rotation of the earth brought the other side into view, I did see one spot that looked recognizable. We seemed to be approaching a mountain. "It's the mount of olives," several voices exclaimed at once. "This is the very place from which Jesus ascended into heaven after His resurrection."

Our descent slowed until we hovered a few thousand feet above the mountain. Then Jesus left the cloud and descended until his feet touched its peak. At this, the mountain gave way as a mighty earthquake rent it in two. The sides parted to the north and south leaving a vast valley in its place. We then settled onto this plain. The solidity of the earth beneath my feet felt strange after the long voyage through space. The utter silence of this once vibrant living planet was eerie. Not a bird called, not a leaf rustled anywhere.

And then I saw him. Over a distant rise Satan appeared. This was the first time I had seen his actual form. I did not wish to get close enough to have a better look. Even from this distance I could see darkness and hatred in his countenance. Presently, one by one, I saw his fiends emerge on the horizon. They too reflected the same character. They had been stuck on this miserable, desolate planet for a thousand years with nothing to do but quarrel and fight among themselves and they were in a very ill humor. Our arrival had obviously aroused their evil interest and perhaps their hopes.

Just then their attention and ours was drawn to a brilliant object in the sky. At first it appeared to be a brilliant star, but as it drew nearer the earth, we gave a shout of wonder and joy. It was the New Jerusalem - the glorious city we had dwelt in for a thousand years, but now it appeared more gloriously adorned than ever.

"It looks so different from this perspective," Andrew exclaimed. "Look at the gorgeous foundations! There are twelve layers each made of a different gemstone!"

"And I can see three gates on each side - at least the sides I can see!" Ari stood, mouth agape with his head so far back I was afraid he would fall over backwards. I reached out to steady him. "Yes," I laughed, "there are twelve gates in all. Can you see? Each one is named for one of the tribes of Israel.

The City descended and gently settled into place in the middle of the great valley that was formed by Jesus' descent. The earth was certainly no longer dark! Jesus stood in mighty splendor, robed in His Kingly robes with a seven tiered crown upon His head. My heart swelled with admiration for Him who had once humbled Himself to take on the form of a servant and then suffered the death of the cross.

With a mighty shout that shook the very foundations of the earth, Jesus called forth the wicked from the dead. The earth trembled and shook as billions of graves opened and the tread of the lost of all ages broke the silence that had reigned for a millennium. Cries of anguish and despair now filled the air along with vile cursing. But as the vast crowd noticed Jesus, they were seized with the sudden realization of who He was and they reacted as one. Driven by their overwhelming impulse, their lips unwillingly formed these words, "It is Jesus, the Lord! He is the righteous one!" At this, they all fell on their knees in reverence. The odd thing was, the looks on their faces did not match their words of praise or the position of worship they had assumed. I saw an awful mix of fear, horror, disgust, hatred, and even despair in their expressions.

Jesus turned away, beckoning us to follow Him into the city. As we lined up atop the city walls, we watched to see what would happen next. Suddenly, Matt, who was standing to my right, grabbed my arm and pointed, "Look at that! Isn't that Lucifer?"

I had no trouble distinguishing who Matt was pointing to. It was indeed Lucifer, but he didn't look a thing like he had when we first saw him. Now he appeared very tall and noble with the bearing of a king. Gone was the evil, hateful look on his face. His expression was one that could command respect as a great leader. As we watched, he started moving from one person to the next, healing their diseases and deformities. His angels did the same until everyone was fit and strong and ready to receive his suggestions and to do his bidding. He told them that he was the Prince and rightful owner of the world, that Jesus and all His subjects had taken over unlawfully and that he himself was actually their redeemer. He assured them that his power had brought them forth from their graves, and that he was now about to rescue them from the most cruel tyranny.

"Quite the politician!" my husband observed. "It's hard to imagine such artful deception. Here we are seeing everything as it really is, but all those people really think that Satan is God and God is Satan! Woe to them who call evil good and good evil!"

I shook my head sadly. We had come down from the wall for a while. There's only so much one can endure watching this kind of deception and evil at work. We had a lot of things to do and enjoy inside the city while outside, Satan was busy overseeing the training and organizing of troops, and conducting military exercises. This process took some time as extensive infrastructure was hastily built to support the operations. Provisions were made for food, water, transportation, and energy as well as the engineering of arms and so forth in preparation for the ultimate takeover of the city.

"Mom," Ari whispered, "have you noticed, the gates of the city are wide open! I can't believe it. Why don't they just try to walk in? I wonder why the gates have been left open?"

"It is strange, isn't it, Ari. Both that the gates have been left open and that none of the lost have tried to enter," I agreed. "I think it may be God's purpose to demonstrate that in all that vast throng, there is not one who will humble themselves and ask for entrance. This shows they will always fight against God to get what they want by force. God has not misjudged anyone's character."

Later we observed that much progress had been made toward setting up command stations, communication systems, and generals. There were giants from before the flood, warriors from Old Testament times and from each of the major empires of the world, Alexander the Great, Stalin, Hitler… many seasoned warriors with different ideas and methods of battle, but all strong leaders whom Satan could train and coordinate. Satan consulted with his angels, and with these kings and conquerors and mighty men. They calculated the strength and numbers on their side, and declared that the army within the city was small by comparison, and that it could easily be overcome.

Troops were organized into platoons, companies, battalions, and divisions as they laid plans to take possession of the riches and glory of the New Jerusalem. (adapted from White, The Great Controversy p 664)

Tension hung in the air like static electricity. We could sense that the showdown was about to take place. We spent more and more time on the city walls, watching what was going on. Strong angels were stationed at each gate with orders to shut and lock them immediately if the army outside began an advance.

I was just ascending the wall again after taking a break to think and get some exercise when my sons began to shout from the top of the wall, "Hurry, mom! They're coming! Satan has given the order to advance and they are marching toward the City!"

Everyone stood atop the wall now. The advancing armies looked like a swarm of ants marching from every direction toward the city. As far as the eye could see were fully armed companies marching shoulder to shoulder each under their appointed leaders—an army the likes of which was never before summoned by earthly conquerors. The combined forces of all ages since war began on earth could never have equaled this for size. Satan, the mightiest of warriors, led the advance, his angels uniting their forces for this final struggle. With military precision, in ordered ranks they advanced over the earth's broken and uneven surface to the city of God. (Ibid p 664)

Now Jesus gave the order to shut the city gates and immediately the sentry angels shut and secured all twelve. In the sight of every living being in the entire universe, Jesus ascended to the great white throne set high above the city walls and took His seat beside the Eternal Father. We all followed, taking our places surrounding the throne. Suddenly, intense light like the flash from an atomic blast emanated from the Father, engulfing the Son, filling the entire city and then flooding the whole earth with its brilliance.

The advancing armies halted their approach, falling backward before the shock-wave of light. An awestruck hush fell over the whole earth.

Jesus stood up and looked out over this vast throng of lost souls. From where I stood, I could see tears in His eyes. As the recording angels opened the books of record, a collective pang of agony gripped the wicked as they suddenly became conscious of every sin which they had ever committed.

It was at that moment I turned and caught sight of you. I reached out and grabbed a hold of my husband's arm to steady myself. But I could not look away. The expression on your face was a study. I could read in it all the emotions you were experiencing as you realized just where your feet had left the path of purity and holiness, just how far pride and rebellion had carried you in violation of the law of God. Too late you saw the seductive temptations for what they really were and how you had encouraged them by continued indulgence in sin. You were painfully aware of every warning you had rejected, the stubborn pride which had caused you to turn a deaf ear to reproof. You had beaten back wave after wave of love and mercy until it was too late.

And then, your eyes met mine. A convulsive sob caught in my throat. At first I saw in your eyes the look of a frightened child searching for his mother, but then, your face hardened into a hateful glare. I jerked my gaze away. Hot tears burned in my eyes and my heart felt ripped apart.

With a sudden jerk I awoke. My face and pillow were drenched with tears. I could still see that look as I stared into the blackness of my room. I shivered; suddenly cold all over. After having become accustomed to the brilliant light in my dream, the darkness was so deep. Slowly it dawned upon me: there was still time. Part of me wished it was for real; wished I was back in God's presence. But as I thought of you, I was flooded with relief. Oh, friend, oh, child, there is still time, a little bit of time left to take your stand for Jesus, to let go of the things of this world, to make your calling and election sure. Give Jesus your heart, broken, filthy, sinful as it may be. He is able to save you to the uttermost if you will just come to God through Him, since He always lives to make intercession for you. (Hebrews 7:25)

The Controversy Ended

Excerpts from the final chapter of
The Great Controversy
by Ellen White

In the presence of the assembled inhabitants of earth and Heaven the final coronation of the Son of God takes place. And now, invested with supreme majesty and power, the King of kings pronounces sentence upon the rebels against his government, and executes justice upon those who have transgressed his law and oppressed his people. Says the prophet of God: "I saw a great white throne, and Him that sat on it, from whose face the earth and the heaven fled away; and there was found no place for them. And I saw the dead, small and great, stand before God; and the books were opened; and another book was opened, which is the book of life; and the dead were judged out of those things which were written in the books, according to their works." [Revelation 20:11, 12.]

As soon as the books of record are opened, and the eye of Jesus looks upon the wicked, they are conscious of every sin which they have ever committed. They see just where their feet diverged from the path of purity and holiness, just how far pride and rebellion have carried them in the violation of the law of God. The seductive temptations which they encouraged by indulgence in sin, the blessings perverted, the messengers of God despised, the warnings rejected, the waves of mercy beaten back by the stubborn, unrepentant heart,—all appear as if written in letters of fire. Above the throne is revealed the cross; and like a panoramic view appear the scenes of Adam's temptation and fall, and the successive steps in the great plan of redemption. The Saviour's lowly birth; his early life of simplicity and obedience; his baptism in Jordan; the fast and temptation in the wilderness; his public ministry, unfolding to men Heaven's most precious blessings; the days crowded with deeds of love and mercy, the nights of prayer and watching in the solitude of the mountains; the plottings of envy, hate, and malice which repaid his benefits; the awful, mysterious agony in Gethsemane, beneath the crushing weight of the sins of the whole world; his betrayal into the hands of the murderous mob; the fearful events of that night of horror,—the unresisting prisoner, forsaken by his best-loved disciples, rudely hurried through the streets of Jerusalem; the Son of God exultingly displayed before Annas, arraigned in the high priest's palace, in the judgment hall of Pilate, before the cowardly and cruel Herod, mocked, insulted, tortured, and condemned to die,—all are vividly portrayed.

And now before the swaying multitude are revealed the final scenes,—the patient Sufferer treading the path to Calvary; the Prince of Heaven hanging upon the cross; the haughty priests and the jeering rabble deriding his expiring agony; the supernatural darkness; the heaving earth, the rent rocks, the open graves, marking the moment when the world's Redeemer yielded up his life. The whole wicked world stand arraigned at the bar of God, on the charge of high treason against the government of Heaven. They have none to plead their cause; they are without excuse; and the sentence of eternal death is pronounced against them.

It is now evident to all that the wages of sin is not noble independence and eternal life, but slavery, ruin, and death. The wicked see what they have forfeited by their life of rebellion. The far more exceeding and eternal weight of glory was despised when offered them; but how desirable it now appears. "All this," cries the lost soul, "I might have had; but I chose to put these things far from me. Oh, strange infatuation! I have exchanged peace, happiness, and honor, for wretchedness, infamy, and despair." All see that their exclusion from Heaven is just. By their lives they have declared, "We will not have this Jesus to reign over us."

As if entranced, the wicked have looked upon the coronation of the Son of God. They see in his hands the tables of the divine law, the statutes which they have despised and transgressed. They witness the outburst of wonder, rapture, and adoration from the saved; and as the wave of melody sweeps over the multitudes without the city, all with one voice exclaim, "Great and marvelous are thy works, Lord God Almighty; just and true are thy ways, thou King of saints;" and falling prostrate, they worship the Prince of life.

Satan seems paralyzed as he beholds the glory and majesty of Christ. He who was once a covering cherub remembers whence he has fallen. A shining seraph, "son of the morning;" how changed, how degraded!

The aim of the great rebel has ever been to justify himself, and to prove the divine government responsible for the rebellion. To this end he has bent all the power of his giant intellect. He has worked deliberately and systematically, and with marvelous success, leading vast multitudes to accept his version of the great controversy which has been so long in progress. For thousands of years this chief of conspiracy has palmed off falsehood for truth. But the time has now come when the rebellion is to be finally defeated, and the history and character of Satan disclosed. In his last great effort to dethrone Christ, destroy his people, and take possession of the city of God, the arch-deceiver has been fully unmasked. Those who have united with him see the total failure of his cause. Christ's followers and the loyal angels behold the full extent of his machinations against the government of God. He is the object of universal abhorrence.

Satan sees that his voluntary rebellion has unfitted him for Heaven. He has trained his powers to war against God; the purity, peace, and harmony of Heaven would be to him supreme torture. His accusations against the mercy and justice of God are now silenced. The reproach which he has endeavored to cast upon Jehovah rests wholly upon himself. And now Satan bows down, and confesses the justice of his sentence.

Satan's own works have condemned him. God's wisdom, his justice, and his goodness stand fully vindicated. It is seen that all his dealings in the great controversy have been conducted with respect to the eternal good of his people, and the good of all the worlds that he has created. "All thy works shall praise thee, O Lord; and thy saints shall bless thee." [Psalm 145:10.] The history of sin will stand to all eternity as a witness that with the existence of God's law is bound up the happiness of all the beings he has created. With all the facts of the great controversy in view, the whole universe, both loyal and rebellious, with one accord declare, "Just and true are thy ways, thou King of saints."

Notwithstanding that Satan has been constrained to acknowledge God's justice, and to bow to the supremacy of Christ, his character remains unchanged. The spirit of rebellion, like a mighty torrent, again bursts forth. Filled with frenzy, he determines not to yield the great controversy. The time has come for a last desperate struggle against the King of Heaven. He rushes into the midst of his subjects, and endeavors to inspire them with his own fury, and arouse them to instant battle. But of all the countless millions whom he has allured into rebellion, there are none now to acknowledge his supremacy. His power is at an end. The wicked are filled with the same hatred of God that inspires Satan; but they see that their case is hopeless, that they cannot prevail against Jehovah. Their rage is kindled against Satan and those who have been his agents in deception, and with the fury of demons they turn upon them.

"Upon the wicked he shall rain quick burning coals, fire and brimstone, and a horrible tempest: this shall be the portion of their cup." [Isaiah 9:5;

34:2;11:6 (Margin).]

Fire comes down from God out of Heaven. The earth is broken up. The weapons concealed in its depths are drawn forth. Devouring flames burst from every yawning chasm. The very rocks are on fire. The day has come that shall burn as an oven. The elements melt with fervent heat, the earth also, and the works that are therein are burned up. [Malachi 4:1; 2 Peter 3:10.] The earth's surface seems one molten mass,—a vast, seething lake of fire.

Satan's work of ruin is forever ended. For six thousand years he has wrought his will, filling the earth with woe, and causing grief throughout the universe. The whole creation has groaned and travailed together in pain. Now God's creatures are forever delivered from his presence and temptations. "The whole earth is at rest, and is quiet; they [the righteous] break forth into singing." [Isaiah 14:7.] And a shout of praise and triumph ascends from the whole loyal universe. "The voice of a great multitude," "as the voice of many waters, and as the voice of mighty thunderings," is heard, saying, "Alleluia; for the Lord God omnipotent reigneth." While the earth was wrapped in the fire of destruction, the righteous abode safely in the holy city. Upon those that had part in the first resurrection, the second death has no power.

[Revelation 20:6; Psalm 84:11.] While God is to the wicked a consuming fire, he is to his people both a sun and a shield. [Revelation 20:6; Psalm 84:11.]

"And I saw a new heaven and a new earth; for the first heaven and the first earth were passed away." [Revelation 21:1.] The fire that consumes the wicked purifies the earth. Every trace of the curse is swept away. No eternally burning hell will keep before the ransomed the fearful consequences of sin.

And the years of eternity, as they roll, will bring richer and still more glorious revelations of God and of Christ. As knowledge is progressive, so will love, reverence, and happiness increase. The more men learn of God, the greater will be their admiration of his character. As Jesus opens before them the riches of redemption, and the amazing achievements in the great controversy with Satan, the hearts of the ransomed thrill with more fervent devotion, and with more rapturous joy they sweep the harps of gold; and ten thousand times ten thousand and thousands of thousands of voices unite to swell the mighty chorus of praise.

The great controversy is ended. Sin and sinners are no more. The entire universe is clean. One pulse of harmony and gladness beats through the vast creation. From Him who created all, flow life and light and gladness, throughout the realms of illimitable space. From the minutest atom to the greatest world, all things, animate and inanimate, in their unshadowed beauty and perfect joy, declare that God is love.

God Unframed

By Cameron Shurley

How can Hellfire be Consistent with God's Character of Love?

The villain in any story is determined by who tells it. Jon Scieska illustrated this principle brilliantly in his retelling of the familiar "Three Little Pigs" story, this time from the perspective of the Big Bad Wolf. Turning the tale on its head, Alexander the wolf justifies his egregious faults and amplifies the supposed injustice of others, drawing sympathy to his side as a disregarded victim. In the much larger story of the Great Controversy, Satan's goal is the same: justify his faults, downplay his role, and paint himself as a victim of God's injustice and cruelty. The precarious hellfire narrative offers Satan just such an opportunity. Employing many of the same tools Alexander the Wolf used to shift the account into his favor, Satan has succeeded in framing God, by promoting an astonishingly pervasive perception of hell that is twisted and warped (John 8.44).

The prevalent view of hell leaves its believers vulnerable to sly doubts intended to fester growing distrust in God. For Pete, who grew up in a

Christian home, these unsatisfied doubts led him to question God's fundamental attribute of love. His emerging view summed up to this: "God tells you that He is love; but if you don't do what He commands, He threatens to burn you alive." In this picture, hell appears arbitrary - if someone doesn't follow God's orders, then He flies into a rage, not at the moment of the insubordination, but rather after thousands of years of self-restraint so He can burn all of the troublesome pests at once and call it justice. Pete believed Satan's tale: that God is not always love. A clear study of this issue reveals, however, that God is the same yesterday, today, and forever, that He is just as much the God of love at the moment the wicked breathe their last as He was when Jesus breathed His last. God is the same. We determine our fate.

Satan's goal with his hell narrative is to frame God as a liar who professes to be the very essence of love until one day when He decides to burn His children alive. This is the picture Satan works tirelessly to instill into the mind of the masses - that love and hell contradict each other, tearing apart the very foundation of God's case in the Great Controversy. If God is not love, then Satan is right - God cannot be trusted and has been acting out an elaborate scam on the human race. If God is love, then Satan's theory is proven undeniably false. The battle is between two theories for operating the universe: love versus selfishness. Since love operates with the best interest of others in mind, the fundamental question is this: Is the death of the wicked by fire an act of love?

Daniel 7 seems like an unlikely place to find insights about hell, but the second half of this chapter reveals important details about hellfire. "A fiery stream issued and came forth from before him" (Dan. 7.10). Daniel dedicates two entire verses to describing God's fiery throne. His throne's wheels are fiery. His throne is fiery. Thousands of angels minister to Him, standing in the issuing flame. Then the focus pivots and reveals that a beast introduced earlier in the chapter is on trial. "...The judgment was set, and the books were opened" (Dan. 7.10). The books appear to contain an incriminating account of the beast's words. The beast is found guilty, then he is "slain, and his body destroyed, and given to the burning flame" (Dan. 7.11; Psalm 104.4).

What flame is the beast thrown into? In the lengthy description of the scene, no other fire is mentioned besides God's fiery throne. Either the beast was thrown into a fire not introduced or it was simply thrown into the presence of God. If the latter is true, this means that the same fire that destroyed the beast inflicted no harm upon the thousands who "stood before Him" (Dan. 7.10).

Now certainly it could be argued that the phrase "stood before Him" is not conclusive evidence that they stood directly in the fire. If someone remarks, "We stood in front of the fire," it would be assumed that they were standing some distance back, not in the flames burning themselves to death. But what about examples from the Bible, like the burning bush? God manifested Himself as fire with an intriguing property: It did not burn the bush. Apparently, bushes can survive God's presence; but what about people? On Mount Sinai, when Moses asked to behold God's face, God warned, "Thou canst not see my face: for there shall no man see me, and live" (Ex. 33.20). If "no man can see God and live," then how did Adam and Eve defy these odds? Also 1 John 3:2 adds that "we shall see Him (God) as He is." If God wants humanity to live and commune with Him like Adam and Eve did, face-to-face, then how does He expect to keep us from being consumed by His fiery presence?

Another revelation about hellfire presents itself in Daniel 3. Shadrach, Meshach, and Abednego, three Hebrew friends of Daniel, find themselves pinned between an idolatrous act and a fatal one: Either they worship a golden idol or they will be thrown into one of the furnaces used to smelt the metal to make the statue. Valiantly, they chose to worship God alone, even if that decision led to their impending incineration. But as they tumbled into the flaming furnace, they watched the burly men who had just thrown them in, fall to their deaths from the heat. Yet Shadrach, Meshach, and Abednego were not consumed or even scorched or blackened. To add to the miracle, in this moment of extremity, Jesus appeared with them in the flames (Dan. 3.8-25). How did Daniel's three friends survive the blasting heat of a foundry? Though God supernaturally saved them from being consumed, this could be a miniature example of how we will survive in the fiery presence of God. "Who among us shall dwell with the devouring fire? Who among us shall dwell with everlasting burnings? He that walketh righteously..." (Isaiah 33.14, 15). This verse states clearly that those who walk righteous can survive in the fiery presence of God. Adam and Eve could walk with God and live because they were righteous. The three Hebrews could stand in the fiery furnace because they were righteous.

But why are the unrighteous consumed in God's presence? The sanctuary clearly answers this question. In a sin offering, the fat and filtering organs of the lamb were burnt on the Altar of Sacrifice, because these parts represent sin (Lev. 3.4; 4.3). The unrighteous are consumed in God's presence for the same reason: sin is destroyed in His presence.

God loves, meaning He strives for all to experience prosperity, belonging, joy, hope, happiness, and life - the best possible outcome for their lives (1 John 4.8; Jer. 29.11; Ps. 35.27). Yet nearly everyone has experienced pain and suffering. This is the consequence of sin. Selfishness, Satan's proposed theory for operating the universe, is the source of all human suffering (Rev. 21.8). Greed hurts all who stand in the way of his self-serving goals. Adultery takes no regard for the value of commitment, breaking the hearts of those discarded for another. Murder, whether motivated by lust, loot, or loathing, takes no regard for the life of others, inflicting regret, grief, and suffering on both parties. Selfishness is not a theory for reaching any desirable end. It reproduces itself in the hearts of those it hurts, spreading like a virus to everyone it contaminates. "For all have sinned..." (Romans 6.23). Since God is love, desiring that all should have life and happiness, His objective is clear: eradicate sin.

God could subject the human race to His unveiled presence and sin would forever be purged from the universe (Heb. 12.29). But a problem arises. Because sin is a lifestyle, so intertwined with man's being, destroying the sin would also destroy the person. In the sanctuary service, the fat and filtering organs - representing sin - cannot be removed without killing the lamb (Lev. 4.32-35). The fire of God's presence eradicates the source of pain and death, unfortunately, along with those who possess it. This is against God's nature however, because love seeks life not death (2 Peter 3.9). Additionally, to eradicate sin in this manner would remove all possibility for the human race to ever experience true joy and life, defeating God's entire purpose.

Sin cannot be removed by force. Sin must instead be separated from humanity by being replaced with love. Since the only one who is love is God, to become loving, humanity must let God live within them (Rom. 8.10). This is achieved by getting to know God (John 17.3; 1 John 3.6). Slowly the sin is replaced by love (God), the heart becomes selfless, and the individual begins to experience life more abundantly (John 10.10). This process towards perfect love is called sanctification. As we get to know Him, He lives more and more fully within us through His Holy Spirit. Fascinatingly, in the Bible, the Holy Spirit is represented by fire. On the day of Pentecost, fire appeared above the heads of the disciples as the Holy Spirit filled them with power (Acts 2.3-4; Acts 1.8). The fire of the Holy Spirit conditions humanity from within to finally meet the fire of God's presence without. For example, Enoch spent so much time with God, that He became conditioned to the fire of the Holy Spirit living within him. Finally, God decided that Enoch was ready to meet His fire face-to-face (Gen. 5.21-24). Fundamentally, sin is removed by getting to know God.

If God's love motivates Him to desire ultimate happiness and life for His children, then how does hellfire fit with His objectives? How can hell possibly be an act of love? "And they [the wicked] went up on the breadth of the earth, and compassed the camp of the saints about, and the beloved city: and fire came down from God out of heaven, and devoured them" (Rev. 20.9). The wicked around the city are fully sold under sin, and thus their lives consist of all that suffering humanity endures today, amplified by the complete lack of power from God to do good. The wicked live miserable, unhappy lives as they prepare to attack the city. There is no hope for them to participate in the abundant life God promises because they refuse to ever know God, forever barring themselves from happiness. At this point

God's desire to reunite with them is futile; His gift in vain. To terminate their eternal unhappiness, and to establish eternal joy for those inside the city, God could directly destroy them in harmony with love. But God has no need to destroy them, because He knows that the wages of sin is death.

If someone serves a master they expect to receive wages. "Know ye not, that to whom ye yield yourselves servants to obey, his servants ye are to whom ye obey; whether of sin unto death, or of obedience unto righteousness?" (Rom. 6.16). Romans six likens sin to a master whose wages are death. "The wages of sin is death" (Rom. 6.23). Many people interpret this verse to mean that God renders death to those who sin. But Romans is clear. The master, sin, pays his servants death. Satan claims that the wages for his work is life. "Ye shall not surely die" (Gen. 3:4).

The purpose of the last six thousand years has been to give Satan the chance to demonstrate his claim: that sin brings life. God's rebuttal to Satan's claim states that the wages of sin is not life, but pain and death; but if at the last moment God brings death, then sin is not the enemy - God is. Instead, God waits, giving Satan his last chance to demonstrate that his theory for operating the universe is superior to love. God does not veil

His glory (2 Thess. 1.9). His character of love is fully revealed, because His children have endured all the trials of earth to experience His full glory. The scene is a standoff between unveiled love and unrestrained selfishness. Will sin, left unhindered, bring death or life? That is the question on the table. The wicked wish to never know God and to forever rob the rest of the universe of this privilege by attacking the city and killing its King. The desperate selfishness that rages within them, drives them into the fiery presence of God. In one stroke, they unwittingly purge sin from the universe, and usher in everlasting peace.

No doubt, God's love for them breaks His heart (Ez. 18.23). To watch His children sealing their eternal rejection of life with their own blood must awaken the deepest sorrow and sympathy. The most famous six-thousand year chapter in all of eternity ends in a bitter-sweet resolution. God's heart overflows with joy at the thought that no one will ever again be tormented by the cruelty of sin. Then another thought breaks His heart - that some never were and will never be free by the mercy of love.

For many today, Satan has framed God as the villain. At this time in history Satan's goal is to decipher how many will stand with him on his final attempt to defeat the villain in his own cleverly crafted story. But God's love is as unchangeable as his fiery presence. He leaves the wicked to their own choice: to inflict upon themselves the very hell that God was merciful enough to spare them from. In a strange twist of irony, the righteous live forever in burning fire, not the wicked. Ultimately, the picture of God that Satan framed will crumble into pieces. After the dust settles, the whole universe will recognize without doubt that Satan was the villain from the first day he rebelled in heaven. Hell is God through the eyes of the wicked. Heaven is God through the eyes of the righteous. God is love forever (Heb. 13.8).

Works Cited
The Holy Bible. Authorized King James Version
Scieszka, Jon. The True Story of the 3 Little Pigs. United Kingdom, Penguin Group (USA, 2014).

The Millennium

What Does the Bible Say?

The term millennium is not found in the Bible. It comes from Latin and means one thousand years. The Bible does speak of a one thousand year period of time and many ideas have been promoted as to when this period of time begins and what happens during it. Let's see what the Bible has to say about the subject.

Q: What events take place at the beginning of the millennium?

1 Thessalonians 4:13-17 (all quotes are from the Amplified Bible unless otherwise noted) *Now we do not want you to be uninformed, believers, about those who are asleep [in death], so that you will not grieve [for them] as the others do who have no hope [beyond this present life]. For if we believe that Jesus died and rose again [as in fact He did], even so God [in this same way—by raising them from the dead] will bring with Him those [believers] who have fallen asleep in Jesus. For we say this to you by the Lord's [own] word, that we who are still alive and remain until the coming of the Lord, will in no way precede [into His presence] those [believers] who have fallen asleep [in death]. For* *the Lord Himself will come down from heaven with a shout of command, with the voice of the archangel and with the [blast of the] trumpet of God, and the dead in Christ will rise first. Then we who are alive and remain [on the earth] will simultaneously be caught up (raptured) together with them [the resurrected ones] in the clouds to meet the Lord in the air, and so we will always be with the Lord! [John 14:3; 1 Cor 15:51-52; Matt 24:27-31; Acts 1:9-11; Rev 1:7]*

As we can see from the above verses:
1. Christ comes in the clouds
2. He will raise the righteous dead
3. The resurrected and the living righteous will go up into the cloud to meet the Lord and will be with Him ever after.

Q: What happens to the wicked and to Satan and his angels at that time?

2 Thessalonians 2:8 *Then the lawless one [the Antichrist] will be revealed and the Lord Jesus will slay him with the breath of His mouth and bring him to an end by the appearance [brightness] of His coming. [Is 11:4]*
Revelation 6:15-17 *Then the kings of the earth and the great men and the military commanders and the wealthy and the strong and everyone, [whether] slave or free, hid themselves in the caves and among the rocks of*

the mountains; and they called to the mountains and the rocks, "Fall on us and hide us from the face of Him who sits on the throne, and from the [righteous] wrath and indignation of the Lamb; [Is 2:19-21; Hos 10:8] for the great day of their wrath and vengeance and retribution has come, and who is able to [face God and] stand [before the wrath of the Lamb]?" [Joel 2:11; Mal 3:2; Rev 19:11-16]

We can see that the wicked that are alive at Christ's coming will be killed by the tumult of nature and the brightness of Christ's coming. The wicked dead are not raised until the end of the millennium as we will soon see. That leaves no one alive on earth for one thousand years.

Q: What happens to Satan during the millennium?

Revelation 20:1-3 *And then I saw an angel descending from heaven, holding the key of the abyss (the bottomless pit) and a great chain was in his hand. And he overpowered and laid hold of the dragon, that old serpent [of primeval times], who is the devil and Satan, and bound him [securely] for a thousand years (a millennium); [Rev 12:7-9, 12] and the angel hurled him into the abyss, and closed it and sealed it above him [preventing his escape or rescue], so that he would no* *longer deceive and seduce the nations, until the thousand years were at an end. After these things he must be liberated for a short time.*

Jeremiah 4:23 *I looked at the earth [in my vision], and behold, it was [as at the time of creation Gen 1:2] formless and void; And to the heavens, and they had no light.*

Satan is bound by circumstances. He is not allowed to leave this earth which is empty of every other living thing. There is no one for him to tempt or work with against God. He has to sit and await his fate for a thousand years!

Q: What are the righteous doing during the millennium?

Revelation 20:4-6 *And then I saw thrones, and sitting on them were those to whom judgment [that is, the authority to act as judges] was given. And I saw the souls of those who had been beheaded because of their testimony of Jesus and because of the word of God, and those who had refused to worship the beast or his image, and had not accepted his mark on their forehead and on their hand; and they came to life and reigned with Christ for a thousand years. [Dan 7:9, 22, 27] The rest of the dead [the non-believers] did not come to life again* *until the thousand years were completed. This is the first resurrection. Blessed (happy, prosperous, to be admired) and holy is the person who takes part in the first resurrection; over these the second death [which is eternal separation from God, the lake of fire] has no power or authority, but they will be priests of God and of Christ and they will reign with Him a thousand years. [Ex 19:6; 1 Pet 2:5, 9; Rev 1:6; 5:10]*

1 Corinthians 6:1-3 *Does any one of you, when he has a complaint (civil dispute) with another [believer], dare to go to law before unrighteous men (non-believers) instead of [placing the issue] before the saints (God's people)? Do you not know that the saints (God's people) will [one day] judge the world? If the world is to be judged by you, are you not competent to try trivial (insignificant, petty) cases? Do you not know that we [believers] will judge angels? How much more then [as to] matters of this life?*

The righteous will be in heaven judging the wicked people and angels. Why is there this "judgment" after all the cases have been decided by God? At the coming of Christ He takes His people with Him to heaven. The wicked will not live until after the thousand years when they will be resurrected to receive their punishment of the second death. If you are one of the righteous in heaven, and you discover that a loved one is not there, you can find the reason for this by looking over the records. God has allotted a thousand years to make sure everyone is perfectly satisfied that He has done everything He could to save the wicked and that He has judged righteously in excluding them from Heaven.

Q: What happens at the close of the millennium?

1. The wicked are resurrected
Revelation 20:5 *The rest of the dead [the non-believers] did not come to life again until the thousand years were completed. (These must be the wicked because remember, the righteous were all resurrected at the beginning of the 1000 years.)*

2. Satan is loosed
Revelation 20:7 *And when the thousand years are completed, Satan will be released from his prison (the abyss), and will come out to deceive and mislead the nations which are in the four corners of the earth—[including] Gog and Magog—to gather them together for the war; their number is like the sand of the seashore.* (Satan will be free to resume his rebellious work with all the nations of the wicked who have now been resurrected)

3. The New Jerusalem comes down from heaven.
Revelation 21:2 *And I saw the holy city, new Jerusalem, coming down out of heaven from God, arrayed like a bride adorned for her husband;*

4. Satan gathers the wicked around the city for battle.
Revelation 20:8, 9a *And they swarmed up over the broad plain of the earth and surrounded the camp of the saints (God's people) and the beloved city [Jerusalem];*

5. The wicked are destroyed.
Revelation 20:9b-10 *but fire came down from heaven and consumed [devoured] them. And the devil who had deceived them was hurled into the lake of fire and burning brimstone (sulfur), where the beast (Antichrist) and false prophet are also; and they will be tormented day and night, forever and ever.*

Note: When a person or thing is said to be devoured or consumed, total destruction is pictured. Look at **Malachi 4:1, 3** *"'For behold, the day is coming, burning like a furnace, and all the arrogant (proud, self-righteous, haughty), and every evildoer shall be stubble; and the day that is coming shall set them on fire,' says the Lord of hosts, 'so that it will leave them neither root nor branch. You will trample the wicked, for* *they will be ashes under the soles of your feet on the day that I do this,' says the Lord of hosts."*

Q: Why does it say their torment will by day and night, forever and ever? We need to let the Bible interpret itself. It repeatedly uses the term "forever," "eternal," or "everlasting" for a limited or indefinite period of time. See these examples:

- **Philemon 15** *"Perhaps it was for this reason that he was separated from you for a while, so that you would have him back **forever**."*

- **Deuteronomy 15:17** *"then take an awl and pierce it through his ear into the door, and he shall [willingly] be your servant always ["**for ever**" in the KJV]."*

- **1 Chronicles 28:4** *"However, the Lord, the God of Israel, chose me from all in my father's house to be king over Israel **forever**."*

- **Jonah 2:6** *"I descended to the [very] roots of the mountains. The earth with its bars closed behind me [bolting me in] **forever**, Yet You have brought up my life from the pit (death), O Lord my God."*

- **Jude 1:7** *"just as Sodom and Gomorrah and the adjacent cities, since they in the same way as these angels indulged in gross immoral freedom and unnatural vice and sensual perversity. They are exhibited [in plain sight] as an example in undergoing the punishment of **everlasting** fire."* AMP *"Even as*

*Sodom and Gomorrha, and the cities about them in like manner, giving themselves over to fornication, and going after strange flesh, are set forth for an example, suffering the vengeance of **eternal** fire." KJV*

As we all know, Philemon nor the slave in Duet. could be with his master after their death, David is not still reigning as king of Israel, Jonah is not still in the belly of the whale and Sodom and Gomorrah are not still burning. So, it must be understood that forever means for as long as nature allows. Nothing will quench the fire of destruction at the end until it's job is done and it naturally goes out for lack of fuel.

6. Finally, A new earth will be created.

Revelation 21:1 *Then I saw a new heaven and a new earth; for the first heaven and the first earth had passed away (vanished), and there is no longer any sea. [Is 65:17; 66:22]*

Let's be ready to go to heaven with Jesus when He comes and inherit that new earth He will create! I would highly recommend reading a little book called, ***Steps to Christ*** by Ellen G. White, to understand how to get to know Jesus and accept Him as your personal Saviour. I want to meet you in Heaven!

Notes

Notes

Made in the USA
Columbia, SC
26 February 2025